D1477797

That's a shocking idea....
let's do it!

by

Suzanne Shearing

To my dear son Mark, and his lovely wife Shirley,
with all my love.

Acknowledgements

Many thanks to publisher Darin Jewell at the Inspira Group, and all who helped put the book together, including Mark Bicknell from Church Lane Creative, who brought my cover design to fruition.

Thanks to Jake Briski from Henig Diamonds for his advice, and to the kindly undertaker from the Isle of Wight who didn't want to be named!

Many thanks to all those who read the book and gave the reviews on the cover, and to all my friends and family who have put up with me being a book bore!

I'm grateful to the Cottered Writers group, and the Buntingford Writers Group for their encouragement and critiques.

But most of all I'm thrilled that you're reading my second novel, and I hope you read my first, 'Two Old Ladies and a Secret Child.'

If you enjoyed it and left a review on Amazon it is greatly appreciated. Thank you.

Chapter One

You join me in the bath.

Excuse my nakedness, but this is where I do my best thinking. In the tub.

And right now, I'm thinking about how best to kill my son-in-law.

My darling daughter, Melody, never did have much sense. Such a loving, sweet child, but she only ever saw the good in people.

She was the one who befriended the bullied child at school and worried about me if I had a cold. It broke her heart if an animal was cruelly treated. She was one in a million.

In her teens, she had only one boyfriend, Chester. When she loved, she loved. And despite our warnings and fears, she married him.

As she stood at the altar, looking like a picture book princess, my heart shattered into a million pieces. This man was bad news, and he was marrying my only child.

As the congregation stood to sing hymns, something heavy fell against me. It was my husband, James. His heart couldn't take the pain. He fell at my feet and never woke up again.

I had lost my husband and my baby in one day. But I had no idea what was to come.

Chester was a struggling musician with no money. Melody was a nurse being paid a pittance. But Chester was adamant that they should live in London because 'that's where it's all happening, bruv'.

Melody was always happy to please Chester, so she applied for a job in a London hospital. Trained nurses are always in demand.

But how could they afford to live in London?

Like a mug, I bought a flat for them. I couldn't see my daughter without a roof over her head. And for a while, it was fine. I would visit about once a month, and the pair settled in. Melody made the place homely.

But it wasn't long before Chester filled the place with his musical equipment and loser friends, who would play loud music and smoke dope into the early hours.

My poor, tired daughter didn't complain, but I became less and less welcome as I commented on the drug paraphernalia, pizza boxes, dog ends and beer cans that littered the flat.

She kept quiet about the complaints from the neighbours and letters from the council about the noise and night time comings and goings.

We kept in touch by phone, and one day she gave me the news that should have thrilled me, but it was worrying. She was pregnant.

I tried to persuade her to come home. Maybe I shouldn't have done, but how could she bring my grandchild into a noisy, drug-filled home?

The next time I saw her, she was eight months pregnant and covered in bruises. She had been avoiding me, so I went to the flat uninvited. I found her crying into her cornflakes at 11am, still in her dressing gown. Chester had been out all night. She had no idea where.

She said the bruises to her face had happened when a picture fell off the wall above her bed. Seriously? She had never been a good liar.

I pulled up the sleeve of her dressing gown and saw bruises around her wrist. They had been caused by a patient at the hospital who had gripped her too hard, she said tearfully.

But she had been on maternity leave for two months, and these were fresh bruises.

I demanded that she come home with me, but she said I didn't understand. Chester loved her, but he was frustrated with his music career and was having a difficult time.

HE was having a difficult time!

My fury didn't help. Melody clammed up and wouldn't hear a word against Chester.

Melody didn't call me when she went into labour. Just a text when the baby was born:

'It's a boy. Both ok.'

I tried to call her, but she didn't answer the phone.

Two days later, I went to the flat. Chester opened the door.

'She doesn't want to see you,' he said. 'Don't call again.' With that, he slammed the door in my face. I could hear my grandson mewling in the background. I have never felt so desolate. If only James was still alive.

I drove home in a daze. My baby had had a baby, and I couldn't be there to help her. To love her. To meet my only grandbaby.

Melody and Chester both changed their phone numbers, so I wrote letters which were returned unopened. What had I done that was so wrong? How could my little girl who was so cherished for so many years turn against me?

I didn't even know the name of my grandson.

I decided to park outside the flat one evening and wait for Chester to go out. Melody had said that he went out most evenings. But that night I sat in the car until 1am, and there was no sign of him.

It made me all the more determined the next night. I would wait as long as I had to.

At 10.15pm, he appeared. He sauntered out of the main door of the flats, and went down the road, passing within inches of my car.

I waited until he was out of sight and went into the building. When my daughter opened the door, I was so shocked I nearly fainted. My once healthy, happy child was so thin it was a wonder she could stand. Her hair was greasy and matted, and her face was gaunt and unsmiling. She walked away from the door, allowing me in.

I gave her a hug, and she didn't stop me, but she didn't respond. She was like a zombie.

I tried to be upbeat. 'Well, aren't you going to introduce me to my grandson, darling?'

She sat on the shabby sofa and glanced at a chest of drawers which had one of the drawers half open. She hadn't spoken a single word. What about the chest of drawers?

I moved across the room and had a look. In the drawer was a tiny baby. Awake, but not crying. I gently picked him up. I took him to the sofa and sat next to my daughter.

As I pulled back his blanket, I saw cigarette burns on his arms and his little body. He was floppy and weak. I wanted to cry and scream with fury.

I pulled my phone from my bag and called an ambulance and the police. This was the first time I got a response from Melody.

'No!' she cried, 'He'll kill me!'

'He's already killing you both! He should be in jail.'

'No, it's my fault. I'm no good at anything.'

The vile excuse for a human being had convinced her that she deserved to be half starved and beaten, and the baby should be tortured for crying.

There were footsteps on the stairs. Thank God, the police or ambulance.

The door flew open, and there stood Chester, his face contorted and his dark eyes blazing.

'I thought I told you to stay away,' he hissed.

'Yes, you'd like that, wouldn't you! Then you could torture your wife and child in peace.'

'Torture? What are you talking about?'

'There are cigarette burns on this baby, and just look at the state of my daughter.'

'It's her. She's the one who did it. And I can't help it if she refuses to eat. I cook different things, but she won't eat them.'

'Liar.'

'Tell her, Melody. Go on, tell her,' he snapped.

Melody sat quietly, looking at the floor.

The police and ambulance arrived just a few minutes later. Chester continued to blame Melody, and the ambulance took Melody and the baby and me to the hospital, while Chester was taken to the police station for questioning.

My grandson, who didn't have a name, took months to recover in hospital and was then taken into care, despite my protests. The police couldn't prove whether Chester or Melody had injured the child, so no charges were brought.

Six months after that fateful visit, my daughter was dead. She had been beaten so badly that she was unrecognisable.

Of course, the police suspected Chester, but he denied it and found some friends to give him an alibi, so he walked. And he still lives in MY flat.

That is why I am sitting in my bath plotting to kill him.

And trust me, I will.

Chapter Two

You probably won't be surprised to learn that I have never killed anyone before, so I don't really know how to do it. I've seen a million murders on TV, of course, and in books, but the murderers almost always end up in jail, and I'm not too keen on that idea. Chester deserves to die, but I don't deserve to spend the rest of my life with scumbags, scrubbing prison floors.

The bathwater is going cold, and I'm getting wrinkly. I suddenly weep, thinking of my poor daughter and her baby. Where is my grandson now? I'm not allowed to know. I thought I had the right, but he's been adopted, and there is a huge amount of secrecy.

My only child, my only grandchild, the loss is too painful to bear.

I would still have my family if Chester hadn't come into our lives. Melody could have married a good man and maybe had several babies. How different our lives would have been.

Chester will get what's coming to him, but I have to think this through very carefully.

I could go rushing in with a knife, or a gun if I knew where to get one, but I wouldn't be likely to get away with that. No, it needs to be something clever and subtle.

First, I need to know about his movements, where he goes, who he sees, that sort of thing. I need to get a picture of his snivelling little life. Trouble is, he knows my face. It will be hard to be incognito.

I could do with some help with this, but, off hand, I can't think of any of my friends that I could casually ask to help me with a murder. My friends are normal, respectable people. Well, most of them are.

I could hang about in a rough pub and see if I could get talking to some villains, I suppose. But how would I know who to trust?

No, this will have to be my secret until the day I die. I will have to go it alone.

First things first, I'll change my car so that he doesn't recognise it when I park outside the flats. Then I must change my appearance. I'll dye my black hair a mousy colour and cut it short.

Maybe when I get to know his routine, a method of bumping him off will present itself to me. He might walk along a canal bank, or stand near the edge of a bridge, or too near a railway line. Or maybe I could get a job in a cafe he uses and poison his tea.

If Russians can do it… but then they go back to Russia where they can't be extradited. I think they *have* extradition from Welwyn Garden City.

I wonder how you get hold of polonium. That seems pretty effective, but I doubt I can go into the chemist and ask for a couple of ounces. Maybe I could Google how to make it?

I have now changed my car for something really boring and cut and dyed my hair. I don't think Chester will notice me. He seems to be in a world of his own anyway.

It's 8pm, and I make the 45-minute journey to the flat. I park a bit further up the road and sit in the passenger seat. That looks less suspicious. I have blankets and a flask of tea, cheese sandwiches and a Kit-Kat.

The food has gone by 9.30pm. Now I need the loo. I hadn't thought of that. I'll have to find a pub, but I don't want to miss Chester.

It's now five past ten, and I'm desperate, and still no sign of the reptile that killed my daughter.

It's dark, and there's no one about. I decide to have a pee behind the hedge that surrounds the block of flats. Not very ladylike but needs must. I get out of the car and walk the short distance to the gap in the hedge. All is quiet.

I am ten metres from the main doors of the flats, but it's pitch black. I have just pulled my jeans to my ankles when I am illuminated like a fairy on a Christmas tree. Movement activated security lights. I'm in such a hurry to pull up my pants that I topple over while at the same time peeing.

Then, Chester appears at the door, obviously. I guess you saw that coming.

I push my body as far into the hedge as I can and keep very still. He meanders past me in his usual trance at a distance of about seven metres. He's talking on the phone.

I hear, 'I'm on my way, bro,' so he's going to meet someone. As he disappears, the light goes off.

When the coast is clear, I get up to follow him, but my pants are wet. Somehow my jeans are ok. So, I now have to take off my jeans to take off my pants, lower half totally naked in a public place. And if I move a muscle, the security light will come back on.

I decide to make a dash, or should I say a hobble, back to my car, which is not easy with pants and jeans around your knees.

But I make it and manage to wriggle out of my shameful pants and back into my jeans.

By now, of course, Chester has probably retired and moved to Brighton. I have no idea where he is.

I go home for a shower and a comforting hot chocolate.

Tonight, I'm back again with more sandwiches, chocolate bars and tea, and a bucket.

Just after ten, Chester appears again. I get out of the car and follow him on foot. I have an old duffle coat with a hood and a scarf covering much of my face. Luckily, he doesn't walk fast, so I can keep up at a distance.

I'm wearing trainers, so no clip-clopping of heels. I'm getting good at this.

We walk for about half a mile down suburban streets until we reach a run-down area and a small industrial estate.

Chester walks into the estate and disappears behind one of the units. I hurry to catch up, but by the time I get there, there is no sign of him. There is a door into the back of a unit and a light on inside. He must have gone in there. I go to the door and listen.

I can hear men's voices, but not what they're saying.

Now I don't know what to do. It's bitterly cold and past my bedtime. But I hang on, hiding behind a wheelie bin in case they suddenly come out. But they don't.

Now it's 12.30am, and I am almost frozen solid.

Suddenly, something brushes against my legs, and I let out an involuntary scream.

The tomcat scurries away, and three shadowy figures come out of the building to see what's going on. I turn away and run all the way back to my car without stopping.

Another successful night.

Everyday life gets in the way for a while. You know the sort of thing, washing, cleaning, shopping. Today I'm meeting my best friend, Cassie, for a coffee.

She knows all about Melody and Chester, and I have said many times that I would like to kill him, but she thinks it's just one of those things you say when you're angry. She has no idea that I will do it. How I would love to confide in her. I really do need someone to talk to. She would probably just tell me not to be silly and that it was just my grief and anger getting the better of me. So, we just talk about her varicose veins and the price of coffee.

Maybe I'll risk it and test the water next time we meet.

When I get home from the coffee bar, I look at myself in the hall mirror. My short, mousy hair doesn't flatter my round face, and I realise that I have plummeted into middle age. Grief will do that to you.

James used to say I was pretty, and I guess I was once. Funny how we don't appreciate it when we're young, always finding fault with the way we look. But when we look back at pictures of our young selves, we realise what we've lost.

I sit at the computer and think about the industrial unit that Chester visited. The name on the front was Erih Rofkoorc, with no explanation of the type of business they were operating. It sounds Russian, or maybe Scandinavian.

Next door was a plumbers merchants, and beyond that, a carpet warehouse.

I look up the name Erih Rofkoorc. Nowt. No website, no Facebook, absolutely nothing.

The plumber merchants next door do have a website, and I decide to give them a ring.

I employ my telephone voice. 'Hello, I'm sorry to bother you, but I'm from the Job Centre and trying to find work for some of our young people.'

Well, it's just a white lie.

'Sorry, we don't have anything.'

'Oh, that's a pity. Also, I was trying to contact the place next door to you.'

'The carpet place?'

'No, no, the other side. I can't seem to find out what they do.'

'I don't think anyone knows what they do. They're never there except sometimes in the evenings when we're working late.'

'They're never there in the day?'

'Not that I've ever seen.'

'Have you met any of the people who go there in the evenings?'

'Nah. It's dark here at night. We've occasionally seen cars pull up and one or two blokes go in and out, but that's it. Sorry, I need to get on.'

'Of course, many thanks.'

So, there is no-one there in the daytime. I decide to go and have a nose around.

This is where I need to know how to break in, and then how to leave a bug.

That's if I had one. I go back online. Good old Amazon. One click and my spying device is on its way. I'm quite excited.

I still don't know how to break in, but how hard can it be? They do it on TV all the time with things like hair grips and credit cards. I suppose it depends on the type of door. I wish I had taken more notice of that, but it wouldn't have been easy in the dark.

The bug arrives the next day. It's unbelievably tiny. The idea is that I stick it under a table or somewhere out of sight, and then, with a receiver, I can sit in my car some way away and listen in. Brilliant. But I guess I would have to break in again to get it back.

But first things first. I get in the car at 10am and make my way to the unit.

Chapter Three

It's Sunday, and the other units are closed, so I can walk about freely. I go straight to the door that I saw the figures come from when I was behind the wheelie bin.

It's locked, of course, and it's a strong wooden door with no glass panels. Why did I think I could do this? I wander along the length of the unit. There is a small, frosted window. Probably the loo. The window is shut, but I try to pull it open and amazingly, it gives. Now what?

I think I'm too fat to squeeze through. It would be a tad embarrassing if I got stuck.

But what the hell. I'm here now. I want to know what this place is and why the vile Chester comes here.

I stand on a discarded pallet and reach into the window. The place is not overlooked, so it feels safe. I have my phone in my jacket pocket and my spy thingy in my bra so I can find it quickly. I manage to slither through the gap despite my recent comfort eating and fall headlong into the stinky toilet. I put my head under the tap and dry myself on the grubby towel. Good job I now have short hair. I quickly shut the window and go into the next room.

I think I'm expecting to see piles of money or drugs or dead bodies. It's most disappointing. It's just an empty room except for three old squishy sofas and a table with discarded paper cups and dirty ashtrays.

I take my spy gadget from my bra and fix it under the table with its self-adhesive backing. I have a quick look around the rest of the place; just a tiny kitchen with nothing much in the cupboards and a broom cupboard with no brooms.

I'm hoping that I can walk out of the front door and not have to climb out of the window again, but no such luck. It's been double-locked with a key. I notice another door at the back, and hoorah, it's a Yale and opens from the inside. I have a quick peek to see if anyone's around and leave, carefully closing the door behind me.

Wow, what a buzz! My knees are knocking, and the adrenaline is pumping. I'm a burglar! Or maybe a private eye. Me, middle-aged Verity Brown!

Now all I have to do is come back one evening, follow Chester from the flat to the unit and listen in from the comfort of my car. I can't wait. I so wish I could tell someone. It's too exciting to keep to myself.

I lay in bed and think about what my poor hubby, James, would have said. He would have wanted to kill Chester, too. But he wouldn't actually do it and would be horrified at his mad wife. Mad? Too damned right, I'm mad.

I wonder why someone would go to the expense of renting or buying an industrial unit just to have a few sofas for people to sit and chat. But, of course, there must be more to it than that. They could do that at home.

Maybe they're making porn movies, but there was no camera equipment. Oh my God, maybe they're making snuff movies! Nah, I don't think they do that anymore.

Perhaps it's an abandoned unit, and they just go there to get away from their wives and smoke dope. Boring, but that's probably it.

It's Monday evening, and I watch Chester leave the flat at 10.10pm, and then I drive straight to the road outside the Industrial Centre. I need to be in my car to sit and listen in. I see two other men go in, and then Chester.

I put my headphones on. This is what I hear, clear as a bell:

1st man: 'Alright?'

Chester: 'Yep.'

3rd man: 'Any beer in the fridge?'

1st man: 'No. We're not here to drink.'

Chester: 'Alright if I have a spliff?'

1st man: 'No, it is not alright. I don't know why I bother with you two losers. How can I trust people who always want to be off their heads?'

3rd man: 'Jeez, I'm only talking about a beer!'

This is not exactly the stuff of Agatha Christie, but I continue to listen.

1st man: 'Ok (rustling of paper), we have our target. We don't know why he's a target. As you know, we don't ask. Our job is to (crackling sound).'

Oh no, all I can hear is white noise. Damn this thing. I fiddle with the receiver's battery and connections. Nothing. Damn, damn, damn!

Just ten minutes later, the men reappear and go their separate ways.

So, someone is a target... for what? A con? A murder? A robbery?

What happened to the bug? Did they find it? No, why would they be looking under the table?

This sleuthing lark is not as easy as it looks.

I have to tell somebody before I burst. But not on the phone, so I drive straight to Cassie's flat. It's nearly midnight, and she answers her door in her dressing gown.

'Verity! What's wrong?'

'Can I come in?'

'Of course. Are you ok?'

'Sort of, well yes, yes, I'm fine.'

We both sit at the kitchen table. I suddenly, realise that Cassie is going to think I've gone completely off my rocker if I tell her what's been happening. Maybe I have. But I can't keep it to myself.

I tell her the whole story, and her eyes get wider by the minute.

'Let me get this straight,' she says, 'that's if I'm not dreaming this. You're planning to murder your son-in-law, and you have broken into an industrial unit and bugged it and heard men talking about someone who is their target?'

'That's about the size of it.'

I feel stupid and sheepish now. It all sounds so ridiculous.

'What did you hope to gain by doing that? And how would it help you to kill Chester? I can't believe I just said that. I think you're grief-stricken and not

24

thinking straight. Stay here tonight, and I'm taking you to the doctor in the morning.'

'Cassie, read my lips. That scum murdered my daughter and nearly killed my grandson, who is now lost to me forever. I will kill him.'

'I understand that you're upset.'

'Then help me!'

'What do you mean, help you?'

'Help me to get justice for my daughter.'

'But the police have already dropped the case.'

'I'm not talking about the police.'

'What then?'

'Help me to find a way to do away with that murderer.'

'But that would make you a murderer, and me too!'

'If we do it properly, nobody would know.'

'*We* would.'

'Yes, sweet revenge.'

'Verity, go home and stop being silly. He's not worth it.'

Chapter Four

I'm annoyed with myself for telling Cassie. I suppose you have to have lost a child to understand the raging bull that is unleashed within you by the injustice of it. But now someone knows my intentions, and although I trust her, I don't know how Cassie would react with the thumbscrews on.

But that was yesterday. Today is a new day. I'm just making myself a sandwich when the doorbell rings.

It's Cassie's brother. I haven't seen him in months. He's come to lecture me, no doubt.

'Hi, Zak. This is a surprise,' I say as I wander back into the kitchen. 'Want a sandwich?'

'What sort?'

'Peanut butter.'

'Smooth or crunchy?'

'Crunchy.'

'With jam?'

'Jam?'

'Yeah, you should try it.'

'Really? Very American.'

'They call it jelly.'

'I know, Zak. What are you doing here?'

'Cassie told me what you're doing.'

'Well, she's got a big mouth.'

'Yeah, but she won't tell anyone else.'

'Ok, so have you come here to lecture me?'

'Nope. I've come here to help you.'

'By taking me to the doctor or a counsellor?' I say sarcastically as I thrust a peanut butter sandwich at him.

'Nah. Oh, thanks. Any chance of a coffee with it?'

'The kettle's on. Help me how?'

'To kill this geezer.'

Is he taking the pee, or is he serious? I take a bite of the sandwich and stare at him.

'Look, you want to get rid of this rat who killed your daughter, and I totally get that. So would I in your position. But you can't do it on your own.'

Maybe this is his attempt at reverse psychology. He thinks I'm all talk, and I'll back out if the whole thing becomes a reality.

'Right,' I say.

'I will help you. I was in the army for ten years, so death is nothing new to me.'

Dear God, I think he means it.

I make the coffee, and we sit down in the living room.

'What did you have in mind?' I ask.

'No, what did you have in mind?'

'I don't know. I hadn't got that far. Just something well planned so that I don't have to be locked up for the rest of my life.'

'You're really serious, aren't you?'

'Damn right.'

'You do know that you could get locked up just for having this conversation.'

'Amazing, isn't it. I can go to jail for my thoughts, but the bastard who murdered my daughter walks free and lives rent-free in my flat!'

28

'Ah, didn't know that bit.'

'Will you tell Cassie that you're helping me?'

'Nooh, don't think that's a good idea. This is strictly, and I mean strictly, between us.'

I tell Zak about the bug and what the men said. First, he says that's all irrelevant and a waste of time, but then he says, on second thoughts, it might give us something to blackmail Chester with. I can't see the point of blackmailing him, but Zak says we might need him to go to a specific location to meet his maker, and that could be a way to get him there.

Anyway, we're now having fun. Yes, it is fun, so we decide to go back to the unit tonight and listen in again. Fingers crossed the bug will work. I have always liked Zak, and it's great to have him on board.

By 10pm, we're parked near the unit, just near enough to see anyone going in. At 10.25pm, two of the men arrive, followed by Chester a few minutes later.

I have one earphone, and Zak has the other, which puts our faces very close together.

There is a buzzing noise, and then it clears, and we can hear the voices. Hoorah!

1st man: 'Ok, I haven't got long, the missus is on the warpath, so let's get this sorted. Tony, what have you found out?'

Man 2: (rustling of paper). 'Okay, well, he takes the same route to work each day. He gets the tube to Covent Garden from his home address, which you've got, and then he's in his office until about six. He gets the tube home again, and as far as I can tell, his wife tucks him up in bed, and that's that.'

Man 1: 'He doesn't go out in the evenings?'

Man 2: 'Not so far.'

Man 1: 'Chester?'

Chester: 'Erm, he doesn't drink, smoke or do drugs. No criminal record. Seems clean.'

Man 1: 'Who is this paragon of bloody virtue? He must have some vices. It's not normal.'

Chester: 'Can't find any, boss.'

Man 1: 'Ok. Keep digging. We need to get this sorted by next week.'

There was a bit more chatter about the match of the day, and then they left.

Zak and I look at each other.

'That first guy sounds like a cop,' says Zak.

'They can't be cops. Chester is an out of work musician.'

'They called him boss.'

'I know,' I say, 'And whatever they're going to do to this guy has to be done by next week.'

'We know the bloke works in Covent Garden and gets there by tube.'

'So do a thousand other people.'

'True. Anyway, where is this leading? How is it going to help you get Chester?'

'I don't know yet.'

And I really have no idea what we're doing. But I'm intrigued.

Zak and I are becoming addicted to this drama, but tonight he has to take part in a darts tournament. He can't let the side down. He's their best player. I'm itching to get back to the unit, but it will have to wait until tomorrow. I want Zak to be with me.

He invites me to the darts match, but I'd rather watch paint dry.

Then I go off into a fantasy about Zak throwing a poisoned dart at Chester. That could work. I might suggest it to him.

I have to get back to normality for today. I chit chat with Cassie on the phone about this and that, and I walk to the shops for some groceries. I bump into an old friend at the supermarket, and she tells me about her daughter, and I'm not listening. I switch off when anyone tells me about their lovely family. The pain is too much.

I go home to my semi on the outskirts of town and remember the happy days that I had with James and Melody. I get out the box of photos from the top of the wardrobe and have a good cry. And then I can't stop. I cry and wail like a wounded animal until my shaking, sobbing body is exhausted and there are no more tears to shed.

And then I get angry again. How dare that fucking man ruin my life? After all the years of love and guidance, sleepless nights and caring that I have given my daughter so that she could be a happy, successful adult, and then some slime comes along and takes her life, just like that. He must suffer. He will suffer.

The next day, Zak turns up with a jar of strawberry jam. Ha ha, too late, I've used all the peanut butter! I forgot to get any more at the supermarket. So, he has jam sandwiches.

I did buy some healthy food, but jam sandwiches with thick butter are more appealing than salad. He then spies my biscuit tin and scoffs some chocolate biscuits. Well, there aren't many left, so I help him to finish them off.

He says they won the darts match, and I say if he was that good a shot, maybe he could throw a poisoned dart at Chester. He laughs so hard that biscuit crumbs shoot all over the place. I tell him that we need to think outside the box, and he says that I should stop reading spy stories. But what about people who have been stabbed in the bum with poisoned umbrellas, I insist?

He says they were government agents, and that's the only reason they had access to highly poisonous substances. And there was no point in us dipping an umbrella spike into some deadly nightshade in the garden and expecting it to kill someone.

He gives me a big smile. 'Anymore mad ideas?' he asks. 'At least you keep me amused.'

We're back at the unit, and the men have gone inside. This time we're in Zak's car in case they notice that mine is parked there. We have the earphones on.

There's a bit of banter and then the boss says, 'Ok, let's get down to the nitty gritty. When our target leaves work on Friday, I want you two to use your IDs and get him in the car and bring him here. You should be here before seven. It's dark by then, and the other units will be closed. I'll be waiting.'

'What if he won't come?' asks Chester.

'I'll pretend I didn't hear that,' says the boss, and he walks out.

Zak goes to take the earphones out, but I want to hear what the other two have to say.

32

'Well, he could refuse to come!' says Chester, 'and it's a well-lit, built up area. We can't exactly drag him into the car.'

'We'll think of something. Just think of the money,' says Tony, as he too leaves.

I start to remove my end of the earphones when I hear Chester speak, 'Emma, get me some dinner. I'll be home in ten minutes. I didn't eat that pig swill you left out for me.' There's a pause. 'What if you're pregnant? That's your fault. You should have got rid of it.'

We watch Chester walk down the street, and I fight the urge to grab the nearest heavy object and smash him over the head. Some other poor girl, someone else's daughter, is in the clutches of this bully. It's even more reason to put an end to him.

Chapter Five

'I wonder what the boss meant by "use your ID",' says Zak as we drive home.

'Maybe they've forged police ID cards,' I suggest.

'I can't see Chester passing himself off as a policeman,' says Zak, 'and that guy Tony looks more like a thug from what I could see of him in the dark.'

'Why do you suppose they want to bring him to the unit?'

'I can't think of any reasons that are likely to be good for his health,' says Zak.

We go back to my place armed with a pizza and two cans of coke.

'Do you think they're going to kill him?' I ask as we fight over the last piece of pizza. Most people are too polite to eat the last piece for fear of looking selfish or greedy, but not us. We're both unashamedly greedy.

Zak becomes serious. 'We have a problem here, Verity. This man is going to be kidnapped and maybe murdered. And we know about it in advance. We should report it.'

'You also know about my plans. Are you going to report me?'

'You haven't got a plan yet. You're just a murderer in training,' he laughs.

'I can't talk to the police!'

'Why not?'

'Let's just keep out of this, Zak. They would want to know how we know, and I can't tell them about the bug.'

'We could just make an anonymous call.'

'Suppose they arrest Chester, and he goes to jail. I won't be able to get at him.'

'Well, at least he'd be off the streets.'

'Ok, let's just go there on Friday and listen to what happens when the target arrives. We can call the police then if it sounds dodgy,' I suggest.

'Could be too late by the time the cops arrive.'

'This is ridiculous. We're getting carried away. They're probably just going to throw a surprise party for him!'

I make coffee. Zak laughs, 'Wouldn't that be hilarious if we warned the police about a murder, and when they arrived, a gang of people were eating cake and shouting "surprise" with balloons and big banners saying, "Happy 60th birthday, Cedric".'

That makes me giggle. I realise that I haven't been laughing much lately. It feels good.

Normal life resumes for a couple of days while we wait for Friday.

Cassie is convinced that Zak and I are in the midst of some big love affair as we're spending so much time together. She wants to know if she needs to buy a new hat.

I laugh it off saying that we're both at a loose end, Zak having left the army and me between jobs while I try to come to terms with my loss. We're good for each other.

Cassie thinks I'm becoming a bit distant, and I probably am because I can't talk to her about what's going on. She would call the men in white coats and would certainly try to stop Zak.

Friday finally arrives, and we set off to spy on Cedric's birthday party.

At 6.55pm, a car arrives and parks close to the unit. Chester and Tony get out and lead another man, presumably the target, into the unit.

My heart is racing. I'm worried that if there's any violence, Zak won't wait for the police. He'll just pile in with his army training. I can't let him do that.

Headphones on.

Boss: 'Pleased to meet you, Mister Collins. Thank you for coming.'

Mr Collins: 'Well, you didn't give me much choice, did you?'

Boss: 'Yes, sorry about that. Won't you take a seat?'

Mr Collins: 'Will you please just tell me what this is all about?'

Boss: 'Of course. All in good time. I'm just following orders. Do you have your phone on you?'

Mr Collins: 'I did have, but one of your monkeys took it from me.'

Boss: 'Dear, dear. Monkeys, that's not nice. Give me his phone. Okay, now you will soon receive a call. You will listen carefully and follow the instructions to the letter.'

Mr Collins: 'Who is this call from, and why should I follow their instructions?'

Boss: 'I will hold the phone and put it on speaker. They will explain.'

Right on cue, the phone rings.

Boss answers it. 'I have your man beside me. Go ahead.'

The voice from the phone begins: 'Mr Collins, I hope they're treating you well?'

'Who is this?'

'I'm your best friend or your worst enemy. You decide.'

'What do you mean?'

'If you cooperate, you will find me very reasonable.'

'What do you want?'

'This may seem a little old-fashioned, but I want some money from your bank.'

'Good luck with that. It's all digital these days.'

'Yes, yes, of course. But you still have a cash reserve and cash machines to fill.'

'It doesn't amount to much.'

'It'll do me.'

'I don't have access to it.'

'You're the manager.'

'Yes, but two of us have to use two different keys.'

'I don't care if there are six different keys. You are the one who gives the instructions.'

Silence.

The voice from the phone continues, 'So, Mr Collins, you will go into work tomorrow, and you will meet my man at the back door of the bank at 11am with the money. He will give the password "lavender".'

'Why would I do that?' says a flustered Mr Collins.

'Because we have your wife. And if you contact the police or anyone else, you will not see her again. That is why. Enjoy your overnight stay with my friends, and they will take you to the bank in the morning. When we have had the money in our hands for three hours, your wife will be released.'

'Isn't this all a bit 1970's? Shouldn't you be scamming people online or hacking bank accounts?'

'Like I said, I'm an old-fashioned man. Luckily for you, I have old-fashioned ethics and keep to my word. Your wife is safe and will be returned to you unharmed as long as you do as I say. And don't try to be a hero. I'm sure you don't get paid enough for that. After all, it's only money.' And with that, he hung up.

After that, the men said very little and seemed to settle down for a long night.

Zak and I look at each other. 'It's like being in a 70s TV movie,' he says, looking stunned.

'I'm calling the police,' I say, picking up my phone.

'No, hold on. Let's think this through. You'd have to explain the bug, and you could be done for burglary, and I'm sure bugging people is illegal.'

'Not as illegal as kidnap and robbery.'

A mischievous smile comes over Zak's face. 'I have an idea,' he says. 'I'll tell you when we get back to your place.'

He's quiet and thoughtful all the way home, so I take the hint to keep my thoughts to myself for now.

Once we're indoors with a glass of wine, I insist that Zak opens up.

'Well,' he says, his eyes sparkling, 'how about this? We know that at 11am the bank manager is going to come to the back door of the bank with a large amount of money. Right?'

'Right.'

'What about me being the courier? He doesn't know my face. We could be pretty rich by tomorrow!'

'Zak! What are you thinking!'

'I hope you're not taking the moral high ground. You're planning a murder!'

I laugh. Maybe a nervous laugh. Everything feels unreal.

'But what about his wife? They'll think the bank manager has double-crossed them.'

'How could he have done? They've got his phone and will be with him every minute. One of them will go to the bank with him.'

'Then why would they need a courier to pick up the money?'

'Because they're just the heavies; the big man wouldn't trust them.'

'But if you go at 11am, the real guy will be there too.'

'I go at ten to.'

'I bet the real guy will be watching at that time.'

'Ok, but I could take a parcel, and he'll think I'm there with a delivery.'

'You would be showing your face, and there's bound to be CCTV.'

'I could do army camouflage.'

'To deliver a parcel?'

'I'll wear a surgical mask, sunglasses and a hoodie.'

'What about a burka?'

'Even better!' Maybe it's the wine, but we both laugh hysterically. The thought of big burly Zak in a burka!

We get into the second bottle of wine.

'Just thought of a snag,' I say.

'What?'

'We don't know which bank it is!'

We howl with laughter. What sort of Bonnie and Clyde are we?

'We know it's in Covent Garden,' Zak eventually says. 'There can't be many. We know they're taking him there in the morning, so we could follow them.'

'I suppose that could be done. Probably not too difficult in slow moving London traffic.'

'Come on, Verity, this is not an opportunity you get every day. There would be no reason for anyone to suspect us.'

Normal Verity would have had a fit at the very suggestion, but this Verity has spent so long thinking about murder that being on the wrong side of the law is becoming second nature. And against my better judgement, I'm excited by it. It feels like an adventure after my usual dull life. I have accepted the possibility of being incarcerated, so this isn't much different.

Zak's hyped up. Money has never come easily to him. His army pay was paltry, and he had no savings. He was kicked out of the army, according to Cassie, but he won't tell me why.

He's been sofa surfing for a while and would give anything to afford his own place.

It's a sunny but cold morning as we set off in my car. Deep down, I don't believe this is going to happen. Despite all the wine last night, Zak is as sharp as a pin and full of nervous excitement. He's wearing a hoodie and dark glasses.

As we near London, I pull over into a layby.

'Zak, this is ridiculous. Covent Garden is knee deep in CCTV. How are you going to get away? Wherever you go, CCTV will be covering it. It's not like being in the sticks.'

'There are always crowds in London. I'll duck and dive in and out of shops and pubs, going out the back ways. Nobody will be looking for at least three hours.'

'So, where will I pick you up? Don't forget I'm in my own car. It will be registered as going into the congestion zone.'

'You won't pick me up. You'll go shopping for an hour or so. If you are ever asked, you just gave me a lift into town as you were going shopping anyway. Pay the congestion charge. Then, just go home as normal.'

'Are you mad? How will you get home?'

'I won't go straight home. If they manage to follow me, I need to lay a false trail. I'll get a train to Manchester, say, and go to ground. I'll sleep rough for a couple of nights, and when the dust has settled, come back by coach or hitchhiking. Now come on or we'll miss them.'

'And you're going to be carrying a sackful of money around with you during all this?'

'Banks don't carry sackfuls these days. Will you come on!'

I drive to the road outside the unit. It's still early. Their car is still there. It all seems different in the daylight. I feel more conspicuous.

Eventually, Chester, Tony and Mr Collins emerge and get into the car. Mr Collins is a small man with a comb-over and glasses. He's wearing a suit and tie. Chester looks as slovenly as usual but is wearing dark glasses. Tony is large and menacing.

Chester drives slowly out of the industrial estate and onto the road in front of us. We follow about three cars behind.

The adrenaline is pumping, but we've done nothing wrong. Funny how the body works in anticipation.

It's not difficult to follow them in the slow-moving traffic, but I fear losing them and so get closer and then get paranoid that they'll spot us. I wasn't cut out for this.

After half an hour, we're in Covent Garden. They pull over just long enough for the big guy and Mr Collins to get out of the car. I drop Zak off a hundred yards behind them.

Chester drives off, and for a second, I think about catching him up and ramming his car, but instead I find a car park. I'm so tempted to see if I can find Zak but must just go shopping and look normal.

Chapter Six

I buy a sandwich I don't want and sit at a pavement cafe. This is my fourth coffee. It's 10.50am. Zak will be knocking on the bank door about now. This is madness.

I should have stopped him. I can't bear not knowing what's happening. I won't even be able to call Zak as he's left his phone at my place so he can't be traced. He'll get a burner phone later. I wait until 11.30am, and then decide to go home.

And then I have a thought. The boss may be at the unit with Chester, awaiting the news. I'll go there and listen in.

Suddenly, I can't get there quickly enough. I must know what's happening.

Sure enough, the same car is outside.

Headphones on.

No speaking, just some shuffling around, then:

Boss: 'Did you stay with him all the time? Every single second?'

Tony: 'Every second. I even watched him pee.'

Boss: 'Tell me again.'

Tony: 'I went with him into the bank. It wasn't open and doesn't open on a Saturday, but there was a woman there. There has to be two of them, and they both go in on Saturdays to catch up on stuff they can't do when the bank is open.'

Boss: 'Go on, Tony.'

Tony: 'Collins told the woman he needed to get into the vault as I wanted to withdraw some cash which had been pre-arranged. She passed her key to him, and we went in.

'She went back to her office and shut the door. I gave Collins the sports bag, and he filled it with twenty and fifty pound notes. He reckoned there was about £200,000.

'There was a knock at the back door not long before eleven. The guy stood there in a hoodie and with dark glasses and said, "lavender". Collins passed the bag over, and off he went. Then not five minutes later, another guy arrived and said, "lavender".

'I told him we'd given it to the other guy already. He said he didn't know anything about another guy, and he'd have to speak to his boss. I thought he seemed almost relieved. He soon shot off. And that was that.'

Boss: 'For fucks sake! What's going on? It's a farce! Who's stitched us up?'

He did it! He bloody did it! I sit in the car and shake. It is now real. Zak has robbed a bank. And I drove him there.

I probably shouldn't have come here to the unit. If my car was tracked…

I go home and have a glass of wine. I sit waiting for the phone to ring, but of course, it's not likely to yet. I wish I had gone with Zak.

Just maybe he'll get away with it. I just hope the bad guys don't get him!

It really was audacious. I can't help laughing at his cheek. Just walk up to a bank, say "lavender" and be given thousands of pounds! Maybe tens of thousands.

I so want to know where he is now and how much money he has. I wonder how long he'll stay away.

I suddenly have visions of him on a yacht in the south of France sipping champagne. Manchester, indeed! He's probably flown off into the sunshine, and to be honest, I wouldn't blame him. But I miss him already.

I switch on the news. And, oh my God, there it is! Footage of police swarming all over Covent Garden and a voice-over saying that the local HSBC branch had been robbed after the manager had been kidnapped. A large amount of cash was stolen. No arrests have been made so far. I have to sit down. This is too real now.

It's now Tuesday and Cassie phones.

'You haven't seen my brother, have you? Is he staying with you? He seems to have disappeared.'

'No, no, he's not with me. He said he might be going away for a few days.'

'Really? Where? He hasn't got any money.'

I almost laugh at the thought of him lugging a bag full of cash about.

'He didn't say,' I know I sound lame.

'Are you alright, Verity? You sound a bit strange.'

'Yes, sorry, just a bit tired.'

'Well, will you ask him to ring me if he calls? I'm a bit worried about him. It's not like him to go off without telling me.'

'Yes, of course. We must have coffee soon.'

It's Wednesday and my mobile rings. It's an unknown number.

'Hi, it's me.'

'Hi, you! Are you ok?'

'Never better. Everything alright at your end?'

'Yes, fine. Missing you.'

'I'll be back tomorrow. Can I stay at yours until I get sorted?'

'Of course. Cassie's been asking after you.'

'Ok, I'll call her. Be careful what you say.'

'Of course. I'll get the pizzas and the beers in.'

'Sounds great. See you tomorrow.'

I'm feeling happy now but can't help wondering what could go wrong. They said the money was in a sports bag. That would be easy to follow on CCTV. There can't be too many people walking about in Covent Garden with a sports bag, which must be distinctive with a logo of some sort.

Zak may be free now, but how long will it be before he's identified? He did have a hoodie and sunglasses, but if they put a video of him on TV, someone will recognise him.

And they might backtrack and see him getting out of my car. Now I'm scaring myself.

I go back to thinking about Chester. If it wasn't for him, none of this would have happened.

I should have finished him off instead of following him around and messing about with bugs. I must focus on him now. At least the slimeball won't be getting a cut of the bank robbery, ha ha. Hmm, maybe the gang boss will think Chester is the one who betrayed them and do the job for me. Now there's a thought.

They'll definitely believe it was an inside job, and there aren't that many candidates.

I'll ask Zak what he thinks.

Zak arrives with a big grin on his face demanding peanut butter and jam sandwiches.

He sets down a bulging black bin liner on the sofa. I tell him to put it on my bed so that if anyone arrives unexpectedly, we won't be scrambling to hide it.

We go up to the bedroom and shut the door. He grabs me and swings me round like a teenager. I'm not best pleased because I'm a middle-aged woman and want some dignity. But I'm excited to see what's in the bag, so try not to be tetchy.

Zak opens it and tips the contents onto the bed with a flourish.

'Ta da!'

I have never seen anything like it, and neither have you. Almost enough money to buy this house. Enough money to buy a Rolls Royce or, well, quite a lot of shoes.

'Amazing what a bit of lavender can get you,' he laughs.

I don't want to throw cold water on the moment, but I wonder if Zak has considered my concerns about the sports bag and CCTV?

He says I worry too much.

'What are you going to do with it?' I ask.

'Yeah, that's the big question. I could always put it in the bank!'

'Good idea. I hear the HSBC at Covent Garden is short of a few bob.'

'Sshh...walls have ears!'

'Well, you can't leave it here.'

'Why not?'

'Because I might spend it! No, I don't want to be responsible for it, or you know, be sent to jail!'

'I could buy a valuable painting or something for cash and sell it later,' he says.

'I think the art dealer might wonder where all the cash came from. These days they're very hot on money laundering,' I say.

'It would be better if they were used notes, but most of these look new.'

'If the police have all the serial numbers, you can't even spend it.'

'Probably be alright if it was just spent very gradually on shopping and stuff,' says Zak.

We both go quiet.

'We need to hide it while we think about it,' I say.

'Hide it where? It's very bulky.'

'Well, just for tonight, you could put it in my bike shed. It's very small, but there's not much in it, just some of my junk, and it locks, so it should be ok. At least it would be out of the house. But tomorrow, we need to think of something safer and more permanent.'

Instead of feeling elated at having all this money, it just feels like a big problem. It was typical of Zak to be impulsive and opportunistic without thinking things through. Sometimes that's a good thing, but now we have a stack of bank notes that are probably traceable that could send us to jail for a very long time.

I say this to Zak over breakfast. Yes, breakfast. Yes, we slept together. Get over it.

'Why are you so damned negative?' he snaps. 'I was the one taking all the risks. Now we have the money, and I don't see the police kicking the door in. Why don't we just enjoy it? We could go abroad, have a fantastic holiday, first-class and five-stars all the way!' he softens his tone. 'Come on, honey, let's enjoy ourselves.'

Nothing I have said to him has taken root.

I stand up and put my hands on the table. 'Zak. As soon as we spend any of that money, it will show up somewhere. The police will be just waiting for these notes to appear.'

'We take them abroad and change them. They won't be looking for them all over the world.'

'And how do we get them abroad? You going to carry a bin liner onto a plane?'

'Ok, we drive to France and then to some obscure Eastern European countries and change it bit by bit.'

There's a little bit of me that thinks this might work. As long as we use our own money until we get there...and customs aren't too clever at the French border. I have nothing to keep me here.

'Ok, maybe it's worth a try,' I say, 'but there's something I have to do first.'

I glance at the framed picture on the mantlepiece of my darling bubbly, happy daughter. I have to get justice for her and her son.

Zak looks at me as he crunches on his toast and knows what I mean.

'Verity, I've robbed a bank. And you still want to bump this guy off?'

'Nothing has changed. He killed my baby, and he's walking the streets. You did promise to help me.'

Zak gets up from the table and paces about.

'Jeez, I was law abiding before I met you! Now I'm a bank robber and a murderer.' He says it with a grin and grabs me for a hug before I can argue.

He sits down again. 'Right, well, if you're still determined!'

'I am.'

'Then we need a plan.'

'Why don't we plant some of the money on him?' I say, feeling the evil side of me emerging again.

'What? Why?'

'Because he'll get blamed for the robbery. His boss must already suspect him and Tony.'

'If he goes to jail, how's that going to help you?'

'Or his boss might take matters into his own hands and save us the trouble.'

'He might, but that means we have to hang around to find out. Let's just get going and worry about him later.'

'No. This whole thing started because I need justice for Melody. He's now with another poor girl. She'll probably be next. He has to be stopped, Zak.'

There's a tapping at the door. We both jump.

'Only me!' calls Cassie. I let her in.

'Ooh, cosy,' she smiles, seeing us at the breakfast table. 'Any coffee left?'

'Yes, help yourself. Would you like some toast?'

'Ooh yes, please,' she says, settling down at the table. 'And how's my little brother? Where did you disappear to?'

'Just needed a change of scenery for a couple of days,' he says casually. 'Went to see some old army mates.'

'Are you staying here now?'

'For the moment. What have you been up to?'

'Usual Groundhog Day stuff. Nothing exciting.'

Zak and I have become incapable of normal small talk because we are so obsessed with our secrets. Huge, big deals that we can't talk about.

'Well, we're a boring lot, aren't we?' Cassie laughs to fill in the gaps.

'We're thinking we might go on holiday,' I venture.

'Ooh, tell me more! Have you won the lottery?'

'No,' I laugh. 'Just a cheap road trip somewhere. Nothing definite yet.'

'That'll be fun. I'm jealous! Speaking of winning the lottery, did you see that story on the news about a bank robbery in Covent Garden? Cheeky buggers got away with thousands. I'd love to know where that money is now!' If only she knew she was less than twenty feet from it.

'Yes,' says Zak, giving me a fleeting smile, 'I bet the police would, too.'

When Cassie leaves, we go for a walk in the woods nearby. It's a beautiful day.

'Chester does drugs, doesn't he?' asks Zak.

'Only dope as far as I know, why?'

'Just thinking overdose.'

'Oh.'

Suddenly, on this beautiful day, the enormity of my desire to kill someone hits me.

I don't want to think about it. I want to notice the birds in the trees and squirrels prancing about.

Zak looks at me. 'You alright?'

'Yes. Just don't want to think about anything nasty today.'

'I thought it was your favourite subject.'

When you're overwhelmed with grief and hurt, getting revenge does become your favourite subject. Closure, justice. But sometimes a bit of normality creeps through and all you want is peace. This is such a peaceful location.

But my default position is still to think of ways to avenge my daughter.

We sit on a log. A couple walk past with a dog. We nod and smile at each other. It's all so normal.

When they're out of sight, Zak speaks. 'Look, why don't we go and get that poor pregnant girl that Chester is with and take her to a battered wives home or something, leave some of the cash at his flat, and tip off his boss? That way, the girl is safe, and the boss will be after Chester, who will spend the money and get caught one way or another.'

'But,' I begin…

'No, Verity, hear me out. We can go abroad for a while, and when we come back, we can review the situation. There's no rush, is there. Even if he goes to jail, he'll have to come out sometime.'

'You're forgetting that he's living in MY flat!'

'Well, evict him. That'll mess him up for a while.'

'I would have to go to court. It all takes time.'

We stroll home hand in hand. It feels good.

When we get home, I get the shock of my life. Standing on the doorstep is Chester.

I start to shake. I feel Zak stiffen.

'Stay calm,' he whispers as we approach the house.

As I rummage for my key in my bag, I say shakily to Chester, 'What can I do for you?'

'Have you got my kid?' he snaps.

'No, you know I haven't. He's been adopted.'

'Who by?'

'I have no idea.'

His eyes flare. 'Liar!'

Zak steps in. 'I think you'd better go.'

'Mind your own business, idiot. This has nothing to do with you.'

'I'm making it my business. Now move!'

'I'll move when I know where my kid is.'

'That'll be the one you loved so much you burned him with cigarette ends.' My temper's rising.

'That was your dear daughter who did that. Stupid scrubber,' he says.

I lunge at him, and Zak stops me and grabs Chester by the throat. He motions for me to open the door. My hands are shaking so much it takes a minute, but then the two men are inside, and Zak is beating the living daylights out of Chester. He's in a furious frenzy.

And soon Chester lies still.

Chapter Seven

'Is he dead?' my voice comes out in a whisper.

Zak is moving about the room shaking his wrists and trying to calm down. He goes to Chester and feels for a pulse in his neck.

'He's alive.'

I gasp.

Zak still has his fingers on Chester's neck. 'Not anymore,' he says.

'He's dead?'

'You're welcome,' says Zak, as he flops onto the sofa. I flop next to him. We both stare at Chester.

Tears start falling down my face. They're not for Chester. They're shock and relief and sorrow and grief and love for my daughter.

Zak looks at me. 'What a total shit that man was. We've done the world a favour.' He sees my tears and gives me a hug. 'It's over, sweetheart.'

But it's not over. It's just the beginning.

'What will we do with him?' I ask, shuddering.

'Leave that to me. I'll put him in the back garden under that old tarpaulin for now, and tonight I'll get rid of him.'

So now we have a stash of money and a dead body to hide. This is getting ridiculous. And it's not as if we went looking for either really. Ok, we did.

I pick up the picture of Melody. 'You can rest in peace now, sweetheart. The monster won't be bothering anyone anymore.'

Zak comes back from the garden and pours us both a drink.

'Not quite how I expected this day to end,' he says.

'No, I just can't believe it.'

'But you're not sorry, right?'

'No, it's just such a shock.'

'Well, now we can get away and relax abroad.'

'But what if someone saw him come here, or the argument on the doorstep...and then we go away? It'll look suspicious.'

'You are such a worry guts.'

'We could report it and say that it was self-defence, that he came here looking for a fight.'

'Verity, do you seriously want the police crawling all over the place?'

He's right. Let's just get away. I can't wait to start packing and get away from this house. I'm not sure I'll ever want to live here again.

After dark, we put Zak's car into the garage and enter from the back door with the body, which we put in the boot.

Zak tells me to stay at home, but I want to go with him. He drives for about five miles down country lanes to some woods next to a pig farm. Why are bodies always dumped in woods? Or under patios? I think he could be more imaginative.

'Have you got a spade? Are you going to bury him?' I ask, almost sarcastically. I don't know why.

He looks at me. He's irritated.

'What would you like me to do, hang him from a tree? Have you got a better idea?'

'Yes, chop him up and feed him to the pigs.'

Zak looks horrified.

'I'm joking!'

'Sometimes I worry about you,' he says, getting out of the car.

I know what he means. I worry about myself. How could I even think a thing like that?

'I blame it on TV,' I say, trying to lighten the mood.

Zak drags Chester from the boot and throws him over his shoulder in a sort of fireman's lift.

I decide to stay in the car. I don't want to irritate him anymore, and I need to keep a lookout. He walks off into the distance and out of sight.

It's a good half hour before he returns. Without speaking, he gets in the car and drives home.

The strange thing is that I have been obsessing about killing Chester for so long that I don't know what to think about now. I have to retrain my mind to think about our new challenges, going abroad, changing the money and staying free.

We're both exhausted and fall into a deep sleep. In the morning, it all seems unreal.

I feel as if I'm living in some strange dream. Did Verity Brown, ordinary member of the law-abiding middle classes, really get involved in robbery and murder?

Suddenly, I can't breathe. No, I really can't breathe. I think I'm having a heart attack. Where's Zak?

He comes into the bedroom with a cup of tea, takes one look at me, puts the tea down and rushes over.

'What is it? What's the matter?'

I gasp for air. He rushes downstairs and comes back with a paper bag.

'Breathe into that; do it now,' he says as he covers my mouth and nose. I try to pull away from this lunatic, but gradually I can breathe again, and I sit down, shaking from head to toe.

'You were having a panic attack. You're alright now. Drink your tea, and don't do that to me again!'

We spend the day packing and preparing for our trip. We book our ferry crossing and set off at dawn the next day.

It's a huge risk. We have no idea about customs checks at either end. But there's no point in having all this money if we can't spend it. And we want to get out of the country just to feel safer.

Luckily, we both have up-to-date passports, and we now look and feel like a couple.

Online it says that we have to declare that the car has no goods in it. That it's empty. Who goes on holiday with an empty car?

There is nowhere to hide this amount of money in an old Ford Mondeo, so we pack it into a large suitcase along with the other bags and hope for the best. If we're caught, we're caught. A trained sniffer dog could sniff out this money from Cornwall!

60

Strangely, I manage to relax as we board the ferry. They just wave us on, and we have no problems at all.

I'm actually beginning to enjoy myself, and Zak is his usual laid-back self. It's like being on a cruise. We have a good meal of posh fish and chips and a bottle of wine.

By the time we've finished eating, we're in Calais. I guess we look like any other pale-faced English couple as no one gives us a second glance, and we're on our way.

After a couple of hours of motorway driving, we stop for a coffee.

We look at each other across the table, both looking and feeling a bit stunned.

'What the fuck are we doing?' asks Zak.

He beat me to it. What the fuck ARE we doing?

'We're going on an adventure with a shedload of money,' I say cheerfully.

'It'll take us until we're ninety to change up all this cash,' he says.

'Well, that will keep us in luxury in our retirement home then.'

'Seriously, Verity, we can't just wander around Europe like two lost souls for the rest of our lives.'

'Maybe not for the rest of our lives, but we've only just begun this road trip. It'll be fun!'

My phone rings. It's Cassie. Damn, meant to get a burner phone.

'Hi, lovers!'

'Hi, Cassie. How are you?'

'You've gone away at the wrong time! You're missing all the excitement.

'A body's been found in the woods. You know the place, near the pig farm.

'They're saying it's murder. I went to have a nose, but it was swarming with police and taped off. A young cop told me it's a man, but that's all I could find out. Oh yes, and they said that he had a big wad of cash on him, so it wasn't a robbery.'

For a moment I can't speak.

'Sorry, Cassie, bad reception, I can hardly hear you.' With that, I finished the call.

I turned to Zak. 'Did you plant cash on Chester?'

'Yep.' He had heard the call.

'They're all over it now.'

'Of course, they are. What did you expect?'

'Once they find out...oh no, I just thought of something!'

'What?'

'Once they find out that the money came from the robbery, and the identity of Chester, they'll find out about the industrial unit and find the bug with my fingerprints all over it.'

'You didn't wipe it?'

'I don't think so.'

'Well, you're taking a lot of leaps there. They might never know about the unit.'

'And then they'll find out about what Max did to Melody and want to talk to me!'

'For crying out loud, Verity, calm down or you'll have another panic attack. What if they want to talk to you? You're not there, and even if you were, there's nothing they can do. You didn't do it.'

'Did you wipe the notes down?'

'No, I was wearing gloves.'

62

'But I had handled them.'

'Do the police have your fingerprints?'

'No.'

'Ok, new rules. We are now on holiday. Most people could only dream of this situation. We have money, no responsibilities, lots of free time, and we have each other. And we love each other, don't we?'

Oh my God, he loves me!

'Of course.'

'Right. No more worrying. Of course, anything could happen, but no amount of worrying will change that, so let's just enjoy ourselves. We'll stop at the next five-star hotel and make love until the morning!'

We both laugh. Well, let's face it, we're lucky if our lovemaking takes more than three minutes.

It's 8am, and there's a knock on the hotel room door.

'Apologies,' says the manager. 'But we noticed that your car had gone this morning and came to check that you were still here.'

Zak leaps out of bed stark naked and looks out of the window into the car park. Sure enough, no sign of the car.

'No one would steal my old Mondeo,' he splutters, 'why would they when the car park is full of Mercs and Beamers?'

'Sadly, monsieur, with respect, older cars are easier to steal for joy riders.

'Sorry again, sir, but we don't lock the car park as people come and go at all hours. But we do check which cars are using our car park.'

'Yes, don't worry.' Zak manages a watery smile. And the man leaves.

'Maybe it's no bad thing,' I say, trying to see the positive side. 'We'll get a new car and be less traceable.'

Zak slumps on the bed. 'And what do we use to buy the new car?'

'You didn't leave the money…?'

'Why not? It wasn't on view, and who would steal that old banger? Don't answer that.'

'So, do we report it to the police?'

'Are you mad?'

'The car may have been dumped if it was joy riders. We need to get the car back.'

'And how do we explain the money?'

'Do you honestly believe it would still be there?' I ask.

'It's possible, if they didn't check the boot. And if it is, our prints will be all over it, and it's English money!'

I'm really worried now. 'What are we going to do without the car or the money?'

'I kept a grand in used notes back, thank God.'

'That's good, but it won't last long.'

'It'll at least pay for the hotel until we decide what to do.'

We're in the dining room having breakfast when the manager appears at our table.

'Excuse me for interrupting your meal, but as you are guests in our country and don't have the language, I took the liberty of informing the gendarmerie about your car.

'They have just telephoned me to say that the car was found this morning about a mile from here. Probably somebody used it to get home.

'It has been taken to the commissariat, and you can collect it from there. You will need your ID. Let me know if you want me to call a taxi for you.'

'Thank you, thank you so much,' I say, and the man goes.

Zak sits there looking stunned with bits of croissant on his chin.

'I'm assuming the commissariat is the police station?' he says to me.

'I guess so.'

'Well, it should be straight forward. We have ID. Unless the cash is still there, of course.'

Suddenly, I start laughing. It's all so ridiculous and unbelievable. We have the proceeds of a bank robbery in our car, and now the car's at the police station. Maybe it's nerves, but I can't stop, and Zak, after wondering for a moment if I'd lost the plot, starts laughing too. In fact, we both become hysterical, which is not ideal in a hotel dining room, and some diners also start to giggle, while others look at us with disdain.

We both get up and rush back to our room, still spluttering coffee and croissants as we go.

As we calm down, Zak says, 'What was so funny?'

That sets me off again. No idea. You just had to be there.

We decide that only one of us should go to the police station in case we're walking into a trap. The other should leave the hotel and wait in a coffee bar.

At first it, seems obvious that Zak should be the one to go. It would be the gentlemanly thing to do. But then we argue that maybe a woman would be less likely to be suspected of wrongdoing.

We eventually decide that a middle-aged couple is the best image to present, so we both go.

We hold hands as we walk into the modern concrete and glass building. The desk officer speaks good English.

He tells us that he will take us to the car which is in their car park. He wants to know if anything is missing from it. Is this routine, or do they know?

The car looks fine, no damage. We look around inside, all fine. Then the officer lifts the boot lid. The suitcase is still there.

'You'd better open it, monsieur, to make sure nothing has been stolen.'

'Um, I haven't got the key with me,' says Zak.

'I think I can find a key that will do the job,' says the gendarme, 'I won't be a minute'.

He disappears back into the police station.

'Now what!' I hiss.

'Let's get out of here.'

Zak jumps in the car and starts the engine. 'Quick, get in.' I slide in beside him.

'This is a police yard. You won't be able to drive out!' I shout.

Just then a police car drives towards the large iron gates, and they automatically open. Zak speeds up behind him and manages to get through before the gates close.

He drives like a maniac until I tell him to calm down and pull over somewhere so we can check the suitcase. He pulls into a lorry park, and we rush to open the case. The money has gone. There is a note:

Ce n'etait pas tres intelligent, n'est-ce pas, mais merci. Je peux acheter ma propre voiture maintenant!

We get back in the car without saying a word. Zak just stares at the note. My schoolgirl French tells me it says basically, 'That wasn't very clever, but thanks, I can afford my own car now!'

Chapter Eight

At least we have the car and a few hundred quid. It's a warm day, and we find a beauty spot to sit and think about what to do next.

I have a feeling of overwhelming relief that we no longer have to try to change the money or hide it. I think that secretly Zak feels that way to some extent, but a few of his dreams have been crushed, and he looks desolate.

'We'll have to go home,' he says sadly.

'Would that be so bad?' I ask.

'Yes! I was looking forward to a road trip. And I'm not looking forward to going back to the scene of the crime.'

'Self-defence is not a crime.'

'Beating the shit out of someone and then burying them is. And then there's the small business of the bank robbery.'

'You didn't rob it. You just knocked on their door trying to sell lavender, and they kindly handed you all their money,' I grinned.

He gave me a look that said, yes, very funny!

'We could always work our way around Europe,' I suggest.

'Doing what?'

Try as I might, I can't think of anything. Bar work and waitressing are out without the language. I could maybe change sheets in a hotel. Nah, rather be at home.

Zak could, well, Zak could turn his hand to most things. But what?

As we sit thinking and admiring views of the rolling countryside, we hear a scream.

A woman runs past us yelling something in French. Then a couple run past as fast as their legs can carry them.

Now there are more people, running and screaming. My stomach lurches. What's happening?

Zak gets out of the car and tries to see what they are running from. More people are coming. People carrying children, all running in fear.

I shout to Zak, 'Let's get out of here!'

He shouts to someone, 'What's going on?'

They shout something back in French, so we're none the wiser.

Zak gets back in the car. 'I'm going down there,' he says.

'What do you mean, down where?'

'I want to see where all these people are coming from.'

He starts the car and goes in the direction of the danger.

'Zak! Please, turn round.'

He ignores me. People rush by, some trying to tell us to turn back.

A large leisure complex comes into view. There appears to be a hotel, swimming pool, tennis courts, children's play area and fairground rides.

There's a loud bang and more screaming. And then we see the problem. A man is running around shooting at anything that moves.

I think the army must hypnotise soldiers, because when they find themselves in combative situations, a look comes into their eyes that you never see in anyone else.

It's a look I have only seen three times in my life, and always from the military.

A Vietnam veteran friend was in England for a visit, and we took him for a sightseeing tour of London. As we walked through Soho, a fight broke out between two men. It had nothing to do with us, and we didn't know them, but my friend stood straight in front of them, with THAT look. He's lucky he didn't get thumped. He had gone into a different zone. It was quite spooky. I won't bore you with the other two stories, but they're similar.

Zak now has that look. He doesn't hear anything I say.

He stops the car, gets out and walks towards the gunman. I shout at him, and so do many others, but he keeps right on walking.

The gunman suddenly notices him and is thrown by the way Zak purposefully strides towards him. He lifts his gun, and I scream and cover my eyes.

I peek through my fingers. Suddenly, Zak throws himself to the ground, and there is a shot. Or was he shot and fell to the ground? Dear God.

There is pandemonium as people start running about. I can't see the gunman now.

I get out of the car to go to Zak. There's a crowd now. I push my way through as I hear sirens approaching. Suddenly, Zak appears and grabs my arm.

'Quick, let's go,' he says as he rushes me back to the car.

'What's happened?' I shout above the commotion.

We get in the car and drive swiftly away.

'Zak, what happened?'

Eventually, we stop at a roadside café, and he tells me. 'I saw a police marksman trying to come up behind the gunman, so I tried to distract him by walking straight at him.'

'You could have been killed!'

'Even trained soldiers miss at that distance if the target falls to the ground,' he says. 'It's all in the timing. Anyway, it gave the marksman a clear shot, and he got him. The police then wanted me to stay to give my details but talking to the police is not top of my priorities at the moment.'

'Did they kill him?'

'Probably. I didn't hang around to find out.'

'Had the gunman killed anyone?'

'Well, we passed three ambulances, so I'm guessing it's not good.'

We drank coffee and had a meal of beef stew, bread and cheese.

It takes a lot to affect our appetites.

We drive on, and as dusk approaches, we check into a cheap hotel near the German border.

I miss talking to my friends at home and hearing all the gossip, but my phone is switched off, and I now have a burner phone, although I have no reason to use it.

In the morning, Zak goes off to buy a newspaper, and I decide that it can't do any harm to call Cassie on my burner. I dare not check my old phone for messages, as it would pinpoint our location if anyone was looking for us.

Cassie is delighted to hear from me. 'I've been trying to get you, but your phone's off. This is coming up as a private number. I nearly told you to bugger off 'cos I thought you might be a scammer.'

'No,' I laugh, 'I have a new phone. What's been happening?'

'Well, that's what I've been trying to tell you. It's hilarious. There's been reports on the news about that bank robbery in Covent Garden. Well, they have some CCTV of a bloke they want to question, and he looks the image of Zak, although he's wearing a hoodie and dark glasses. The way he walks and everything! And apparently, someone rang the police to give his name, and now they want to speak to him. They came here looking for him. They said it was just routine so not to worry. I told them how hysterical it was that he looked like my brother, who was an upstanding citizen.'

'Where did you tell them he was?'

'I said he's gone away for a few days, and I didn't know where. Where are you?'

'Can I ring you back, Cassie, the reception's bad here?' and for a second time, I cut the poor woman off.

Zak walks in and slaps a newspaper down on the table.

'Can you believe this?'

'It's in English! I didn't know you could get French newspapers in English!'

'Read it, front page,' he scowls.

There, staring at me, is a picture of Zak taken on someone's phone as he approached the gunman.

A mystery hero who faced down an armed terrorist is being sought by police. The man, thought to be British, distracted the gunman so that the gendarmes could get a shot at him. The terrorist was killed on the spot after shooting five holiday makers, two of them fatally.

The hero disappeared into the crowd before the police could thank him or get his details as a witness.

It went on to give information about the venue.

'You're a hero!' I say, knowing full well that this is the last thing we need.

'I'm not a bloody hero!'

'You're *my* hero,' I say, throwing my arms around him. 'So, now you have the police looking for you in two countries!'

'What do you mean?'

'Cassie says the police have been to hers, but don't worry, it's just routine, she said.'

He pulls away from me, fuming. 'You spoke to Cassie?'

'Only for a minute. I used the burner phone.'

'And why are the police looking for me?'

'There was a CCTV thing of you in Covent Garden. She laughed it off, said it was hilarious that the man looked like you.'

'Great.'

'Look, if your own sister doesn't think it's you, nobody can prove different.'

There's a knock at our hotel door. Zak reluctantly opens it.

Suddenly, about a dozen voices shout, 'Bravo'! And then they all applaud.

We're stunned. It turns out that there's a conference in the hotel, and many of the delegates are Brits. They've seen the paper, and the excited staff have told everyone that would listen that the hero is right here in this very hotel.

Zak is a very reluctant hero, and this makes them even keener. The man is not only a hero, but he's modest with it.

After much back slapping they leave, only to be replaced, minutes later, by two gendarmes.

'You are very elusive, monsieur,' says the tall one, sounding like Poirot. 'Why did you leave so quickly? You were very brave.'

'Or very stupid,' says his partner.

'It was a reckless thing to do, but it had the desired effect. We need you to make a statement, please.'

'Ok,' says Zak, reluctantly.

'Not here, you need to come with us.'

'Why?'

'People have died, monsieur. We have to do this properly.' He looks at me. 'And you are?'

I can feel my hands shaking and stuff them in my jeans pockets.

'My name is Verity Brown.'

'Are you two related?'

'No,' I reply, 'friends.'

Zak glances at me. What I am supposed to say, lovers? Partners in crime?

'Did you see what happened?'

'Not really, I was in the car.'

Zak is gone for five hours. My imagination runs riot. The Met police have come over and are interviewing him. He's been taken back to England. They've connected him with the murder. He's confessed to everything. They've found the stolen money with our fingerprints on the notes. They've beaten him up. They're giving him a medal for his bravery. Hell, what is keeping him so long?

I doze off for a while and then hear him coming in. He looks exhausted and lays down beside me on the bed.

'Well?' I ask.

'Later,' he sighs.

'Come on, I've been worried sick. Just the bones of it.'

'Ok. It was just a statement about today, and there was a lot of hanging around, and sometimes they needed a translator, but I think we need to get out of here because it won't take them long to check me out with the English police and find out that they were looking for me.'

'The Met are probably checking out hundreds of people who look like the CCTV images. They always get loads of nutters ringing them up saying it's their next door neighbour or their enemy, or even their friend for a laugh. It's just routine,' I say.

'Maybe. But let's get moving.' He starts to get his things together, and I do the same.

I feel that we're drifting apart. Not surprisingly, the holiday spirit has gone. We're lurching from one crisis to another. He didn't need to get involved with the latest drama, but his army training seems to take him over sometimes.

I have no idea where we're going next.

We put our bags in the car and take off.

Soon we cross the border into Germany. Strange how one language can be spoken in one area and just a mile down the road, it is entirely different. I had schoolgirl French but can't remember a word of German.

Zak is very quiet, and I'm hoping it's just because he's tired.

At least they won't have the French/English newspaper here.

It's now late evening, and we can't find a hotel, so we end up sleeping in the car parked in a restaurant car park.

Nobody disturbs us, and we sleep well, considering.

Zak seems more relaxed, and after breakfast in the restaurant, we decide to make for Munich, about three and a half hours away. We're sure to find a budget hotel there.

Money is now getting very tight, especially as we need to buy petrol. This is now a real problem.

Ironic, really, as by now, we should have been changing up our thousands into euros. That was the whole point of the trip, and then there was the running away bit, obviously.

I reach out and hold Zak's hand. He squeezes it and gives me a loving glance. Hoorah, we're still ok.

We stop for lunch before we get into Munich. Well, we get a McDonald's take away and eat it in the car.

'Let's take stock,' says Zak.

'Uh huh,' I say with a mouth full of burger.

'Chester's body's been found… with some of the money from the bank.

'They were new notes, so he will have been tied into that job by now. They will find that he's been living with that poor girl and no doubt uncover the investigation into Melody's death.'

He looks at me, realising that he's sticking a knife in the wound.

'Sorry, sweetheart.'

'It's ok,' I say. 'Carry on.'

'Right, well, if he'd fallen out with the robbery gang, surely the police will assume that they would have taken the money from him. They'll be looking for another motive.'

'Are you sure you didn't miss your vocation?' I say, 'You should have been a detective.'

'There's still time,' he laughs, and I remember why I love him.

He stares out of the car window and eats some chips.

'Then there's the CCTV of me in Covent Garden. I don't see how they can prove that was me. But I will still need an alibi.'

I can't give him an alibi as I was also in Covent Garden, and it wouldn't be rocket science to prove that, as I paid the congestion charge and parked there.

Cassie has already been seen by the police, and so they know Zak wasn't with her.

Zak cuts into my thoughts.

'And then I go to France and get my picture all over the papers within a week!'

'We're not the best criminals in the world, are we?' I laugh.

'Are you kidding? Bonnie and Clyde have got nothing on us!'

He leans across and kisses me.

What would my mum say? Her only daughter kissing a murderous bank robber? I would only tell her the hero in France bit.

Munich is buzzing, like any city. Cars, noise, shops, restaurants. We feel anonymous and safe here.

We book into a budget hotel, but this is going to take the last of our money. We're effectively stranded after today.

We can't ask friends or family to send us money for obvious reasons, but we have to do something, fast.

Neither of us speaks a word of German. Why did we come here? I guess because it's further away from England than France!

We still have petrol in the car, so maybe we have to concede defeat and make for home, although we would still need money to get there.

Unbelievably rich one minute and penniless the next! You couldn't make it up.

Zak is staring out of the hotel room window, looking worried.

'You could always go to the back door of a bank and say "lavender",' I try to lighten the mood.

'The way things are going, we'll be selling lavender on street corners,' he says.

'I could always sell my body.'

'Oh no, only I have access to that!' He grabs me around the waist, and we fall onto the bed. You can mind your own business about the next bit. Just think fifty shades of, ok maybe more like five shades of...oh never mind.

Later, we go for a wander around the shops. Shops are much the same the world over, so we go for a coffee at Starbucks.

'We could always borrow some money,' says Zak, who must have lost his mind.

'Yes, I can see the bank going for that,' I say sarcastically.

'Not the bank. We give a hard luck story to someone who's got a few bob, and they lend us the money until we can pay it back.'

'And where do we find this generous, naive soul?'

'Somewhere where rich, generous, naive people go.'

'Like where?'

'Five-star hotels, casinos, yachts.'

'I don't think a lot of yachts sail out of Munich,' I say, 'and we can't afford to stay in any hotels, let alone five-star.'

'No, we don't stay in them. We just sit in the bar or the lobby.'

'And drink water?'

'Why not? What have we got to lose?'

'Not forgetting that this sympathetic soul has to speak English.'

'Of course.'

We wander, hand in hand, back to our hotel. We have to pass a glitzy five-star hotel on the way, and we try to wander in and have a look, but a doorman politely stops us. Not a good start to our cunning plan.

Over dinner, we realise that our plan must be carried out tonight, or tomorrow we'll be sleeping in the car.

We didn't bring much luggage, but we dig out our best clothes and dress to impress.

We look online for the nearest five-star hotel, avoiding the one with the overzealous doorman.

Now we have to come up with a story.

'We just tell the truth,' says Zak. 'Well, a version of it.'

'What?'

'That we had our money and credit cards stolen while on our road trip. We just need enough to get home.'

'They'll tell us to go to the British Embassy,' I say.

'Well, we'll say we've tried that, but they couldn't help.'

'Who's going to do the talking?'

'We'll play it by ear. Can you squeeze out a tear or two?' he grins.

'That shouldn't be too difficult.'

As we walk the half mile to the posh hotel, the heavens open, and we get drenched.

We run the rest of the way, and our bedraggled appearance works in our favour, because the doorman takes pity on us and lets us in. It also gives us a talking point as we go to the bar, and the barman offers us a towel.

We stand at the bar for a few moments looking around. We tell the barman that we're meeting someone and don't really want to stop for a drink as we're running late.

There are not many people about, which makes it difficult to find an excuse to sit at someone else's table.

There is a woman sitting on her own speaking into her phone, and a man working on his laptop.

In a corner, a raucous foursome is laughing, and another table is occupied by a young family.

We look at each other. Who do we pick?

On impulse, I go to the barman. 'Does anybody here speak English?' I ask with a big smile.

'I do, a little,' he says. 'Can I help you?'

'Erm, well, I just wondered if any of your guests speak English?'

He looks puzzled. 'The man over there,' he points to the man working on his laptop. 'He's Italian but speaks English. Is he the person you are meeting?'

'Possibly. Thank you,' I smile and go back to Zak.

'What are you doing?' Zak asks, looking irritated.

'Finding out who speaks English.'

'We're supposed to casually meet someone and get chatting, not advertise what we're doing to the barman!'

'Well, we can't go from table to table finding out who speaks English,' I say defensively.

'Ok, will you please leave this to me?' Zak gets up and goes over to the Italian.

'Forgive me for disturbing you, but is your name Mario?'

'No, I'm afraid not.'

'Oh, I'm so sorry. We were due to meet a man called Mario de Silva, but it appears he's not coming. Now we are in trouble.'

The man looks up for the first time at Zak. 'I'm sorry to hear that. But I am not your man.'

'No, no, of course not. It's just that…' Zak sits beside the man as he speaks. 'Sorry, hope you don't mind, I've been walking all day.'

'I have some urgent work to do, so please excuse me,' says the Italian as he focuses on his laptop.

Zak opens his mouth to say something else, and the man picks up his laptop and leaves the bar.

Zak comes back to our table.

'That went well,' I say smugly.

'Ok, maybe this wasn't one of my better ideas. I'm a useless conman. You got any better ideas?'

We walk slowly back to our hotel. The rain has stopped, but we're feeling dejected.

As Zak puts our card/key into our hotel room door, a man's voice calls out.

'Sergeant Zak bloody Bently, as I live and breathe, I don't believe it!'

83

Zak swings round. 'If it isn't Corporal Ashton!'

'What are you doing here, Sarge?'

They do a sort of man hug.

'Long story,' says Zak.

Corporal Ashton gives me a smile.

'This is Verity,' says Zak, without saying my partner or my other half or even my friend.

'Jack Ashton,' he shakes my hand.

'Come on in, Jack,' says Zak. 'Are you on your own?'

''Fraid so. Purely business.'

We go into the room, and Zak takes some beers from the fridge and hands them out.

There is a bed, a desk and chair, so I sit on the bed with Zak, and Jack has the chair.

'What business are you in now, Jack?'

'A bit of this and a bit of that. You know, duckin' and divin'.'

'You always were dodgy,' laughs Zak.

'Not as dodgy as you, Sarge.'

'Stop calling me Sarge.'

'Sorry, force of habit.'

'What sort of duckin' and divin' are you doing in Munich?' asks Zak.

Zak never could take a hint.

'Jack, don't answer him. He's so nosey,' I say.

'I like you already, Verity! What are you two doing here?'

'Starving by tomorrow,' says Zak.

'How come?'

'We were on a road trip,' I answer, 'but all our money was stolen.'

'Everything? No cards, nothing?'

'Everything.'

'What are you going to do?'

Zak answers, 'We've paid for tonight, but in the morning, we have to get out. We're ok. We can sleep in the car.'

'Good job you've got a motor. Blimey, Sarge, you always did get into scrapes.'

'Did he now?' I'm curious.

'Verity, you have no idea!'

'Shut up, Corporal, and that's an order!' Zak barks, only half in jest.

'Look, I won't keep you guys up,' says Jack, 'but if you meet me for breakfast in the morning at eight, I might have a business proposition for you.' With that, he goes to the door.

'Can't you tell us now?' says a desperate Zak.

Jack puts a finger to the side of his nose, winks, and leaves.

Jack is definitely dodgy, but so are we, so I'm keen to hear what he has to say. Zak says he's a bit of a wide boy, but there's no malice in him, and he's totally reliable and loyal.

He can't think what he's doing in Germany, but maybe we'll find out tomorrow.

We go to bed in a more hopeful frame of mind.

Jack is at the breakfast table before us and is already tucking into bread rolls with jam and honey, and there is cheese and some sort of sausage as well. He's pleased to see us, and even pulls up a chair for me.

The breakfast is self-service, and Jack has made sure that he has put enough on the table for all of us.

'Mornin', Sarge and Missus Sarge,' he grins.

'Morning, Jack,' we chorus.

'So, what's this business plan?' asks Zak.

'Jeez, Sarge, you don't change. Straight in there. Ok, here it is. You want to get home, right?'

'Not really, but we don't have much choice,' I say.

'Okay, I have to fly back tomorrow but supposing I pay for your journey home, petrol, food, overnight stay and the crossing, and in return, you take some of my stuff back that I can't take on the plane?'

'What sort of stuff? Guns, toothpaste?' says Zak.

'Ok, not strictly kosher, I'll admit. But you don't need to know.'

'Oh yes, we do!' snaps Zak.

'Oh no, you don't,' laughs Jack in pantomime fashion.

'Look,' he says, 'that's the deal. You take a locked box back with you with all your other stuff in the back of your car. They never check on the ferries. Then we meet in London next week, you hand over the unopened box with its contents intact, and I give you a grand. I can't say fairer than that.'

'And I go to jail for a lousy grand!'

'Take it or leave it, Sarge. It's just an idea.'

Zak and I go back to our room to discuss it, while Jack continues to scoff in the dining room.

Zak paces up and down. 'Do we have any choice? We're penniless.'

'If we're going home, we could just use our cards. It doesn't matter if anyone knows our whereabouts. We wouldn't be on the run anymore,' I say, feeling as if this is a light bulb moment, but really so bloody obvious.

Zak looks at me. He's thinking about it.

'Um, but we wouldn't want to be picked up here or in France. We don't know how far the police have got. That's the trouble; ok, it might be that we're just on a routine list of enquiries, but if we are number one suspects, they would be quick off the mark as soon as we show ourselves by using our cards or phones.'

'But we're in enough trouble without smuggling God knows what into the UK,' I say.

Zak does some more pacing.

He gives me a grin, 'We could always take Jack's box and dump it before we get on the ferry,' he says mischievously.

But I know he wouldn't do that to a friend, and so does he.

'So, how do we explain the box if we do get caught?' I want to know.

'We make sure we don't get fingerprints on it and deny all knowledge.'

'Nobody would believe that.'

'Maybe not. But they'd have to prove our intent.'

'Does that mean we're doing it, then?'

'It's up to you. I don't think we have any choice. I don't want to be nicked on the continent. We could be locked up for ages before we get extradited. I'd rather be on home turf. Of course, we could be home free, and nothing happens.'

'Oh well, in for a penny, in for a pound.'

I give Zak a hug, and we go back to the dining room to break the news to Jack.

Only Jack isn't there. A waitress sees us looking for him and brings an envelope.

Inside is a note:

Sorry Sarge, had to get going. The box is in a locker at Munich station. I'm enclosing the key. It has the locker number on it. This must be collected within 72 hours or they confiscate any contents. See you next week. Call me on the number on the back of this note when you get home. Bon voyage!

'Cheeky bugger! Takes a lot for granted. We hadn't even said we'd do it!' says Zak.

As I glance toward the window, I see Jack just disappearing. Making sure we got the envelope and couldn't say no, I guess.

I don't say anything as Zak might run after him, and I'm intrigued now. Hang on, though, what about the money to get home?

Zak turns the note over. As well as a phone number there is another message.

P.S. You will also find enough euros in the locker to get you home.

Suddenly, we can't wait. I'm always excited in movies when something is hidden in a railway locker. And Zak just wants to get his hands on some cash so we can get moving.

I feel conspicuous as we enter the station, but it's busy, and nobody is taking any notice of us.

We find the locker quite easily, and Zak opens it. Inside is a green duffle bag that takes up most of the space. Inside it is a metal box, a sort of miniature safe. Very heavy. There's also an envelope in the bag with 1500 euros in it. If we're careful, it should get us home, but it's not exactly champagne money.

We take the bag back to our hotel room and have a good look at the box. We so want to open it. We shake it about, but it gives us no clue as to what's inside.

It measures about 30cm x 38cm x 20cm and needs some kind of a round key. There is no way you could smash it open with a hammer or lever it with a screwdriver. It's as solid as a rock. It doesn't smell of anything.

We're dying of curiosity. But for now, at least, there's nothing we can do but put it back in the duffle bag and get going.

Zak has told me not to, but I can't resist. I ring Cassie on my burner phone when he's packing our stuff into the car. I think it's safe enough as we're on the move all the time, and I'll take the battery out afterwards.

'Verity! Where've you been? Your phone's been switched off. I've been worried.'

'We're fine. You mustn't worry.'

'Well, you'll never guess what. You know that body they found in the woods? It was only your Melody's husband, Chester! I've been dying to tell you. Somebody's beaten you to it!'

I feel as though I've been punched in the stomach. Of course, I knew that, but I had somehow managed to hide it away in the back of my brain, and now it had become real again.

'Oh my God,' I say. 'What a shock. Do they know who did it?'

'Well, no arrests have been made or else it would have been in the papers.'

'He upset a lot of people,' I say. 'Could have been any of his enemies.

'Anyway, we're on our way home, so I'll see you in a few days. We can talk about it then.'

I collect the rest of our bits and pieces from the hotel room, and we start on our journey home.

Chapter Nine

It's almost a ten-hour journey to Calais, so we have one stopover. We're not looking forward to going home but can't think of an alternative.

The mysterious box has to go everywhere with us. Can't risk leaving that in the car!

We don't talk much, both in our own thoughts.

Our journey is uneventful, and we finally arrive at Calais.

A customs officer approaches us. He glances around the car.

'Been on a booze cruise?'

'No,' smiles Zak, 'no booze or fags.'

'That must be a first,' he says, opening the boot.

'So, where have you been?'

'Just a road trip, France and Germany,' says Zak politely.

The customs man looks hard at Zak. 'You look familiar. I've seen your face before.'

'Maybe on the way over,' I say.

'Wait here,' he says and walks away.

We look at each other. What now? Has Zak's face been circulated as wanted?

What if they open the box?

The man reappears with another customs officer. They both look at Zak.

The other man says, 'Yes, that's him,' and to Zak, 'Please leave the car here and come with me.'

My stomach is doing somersaults. The colour drains from Zak's face.

'What's the problem?' asks Zak.

'Follow me, please, both of you.'

The first customs man is walking some way ahead of us and talking on his radio.

The second one stays with us but won't be drawn on what's happening.

Everything starts flashing through my mind: the unit, the bank manager, Chester, Melody, lavender, the money, the fight in my house, the burial in the woods, the secret box.

We walk for a long way, past several customs buildings. Then we are taken into an office and told to sit down. More uniformed people arrive. They are all looking at us. I'm holding back the tears. Then even more officers trickle in. Dear God, this is terrifying, but we *are* talking about bank robbery and murder, so I shouldn't be surprised. But I'd kind of got used to feeling that the trouble was all behind us. Wishful thinking, I guess.

When everyone is in the room, customs man number two raises his arm, and they all start singing, 'For he's a jolly good fellow, for he's a jolly good fellow, for he's a jolly good fellow, and so say all of us.'

A lady then walks in with a tray full of glasses of champagne.

Customs man two says, 'You stood in front of an armed terrorist and saved dozens of lives. You are a true hero, and you left before you could be properly congratulated, so at least before you leave our country, we would like to raise a toast to you and your lovely lady. Thank you!'

There's enthusiastic applause. I think if I was not sitting down, I would faint. Zak is white and speechless.

The man continues, 'We don't want to hold you up as the ferry is about to leave, but we have put a crate of champagne in your car as you had no booze!'

There's much back slapping and cheering as we leave.

We get back into the car and drive onto the ferry.

I feel weak and shaky from the adrenaline rush. We get a coffee and sit down. Zak bursts out laughing. My nerves are so shot that I giggle too.

'I thought I was going down for twenty years, and I get a champagne reception!' he laughs.

I have to shush him before he tells the whole ferry.

Cassie has cleaned the place, watered the plants and put food in the fridge.

It's a cold day, and she's put the heating on.

Good to come back to a warm house. Cassie can always be relied upon, but she can be a bit full on.

We were half expecting to see a police cordon around the house or snipers on the roof, so it's almost an anti-climax to see everything looking normal.

As I walk into the living room, I'm horrified to see bloodstains on the carpet. The whole horrible fight comes back to me. How had I not noticed the stains? I guess we were in such a hurry to get away that everything was a blur.

Zak was oblivious, but I pointed them out to him.

'We won't get those out,' he says. 'The whole carpet will have to go.'

He starts moving the furniture so that he can pull the carpet up. I start to unpack, wondering if there is any other blood that I've missed.

I'd almost forgotten about the mystery box, but at least we've brought it back safely, so we'll get a grand from Jack. It's so frustrating not to know what's in it. I'm determined to find out. There must be a way.

Zak has pulled up the carpet and dragged it into the garage. How the hell are we going to get rid of that huge thing?

Zak says he needs to get rid of it now, along with the tarpaulin that he had covered the body with. He manages to bend the carpet in half and with the help of an old roof rack, ties it to his car.

He takes off, and I inspect the house for any more stains. I've seen it on TV. Sometimes the stains are miniscule and can't be seen by the naked eye, so I must clean everything.

Oh no, I just had a thought. Cassie's been in to clean and water the plants. Did she notice the stains?

I'll say I had a nosebleed if she says anything. I must remember to tell Zak.

I put my reading glasses on and examine every inch of the living room and everywhere the body went. Nowt. So, hopefully okay.

I go back to the mystery box which is now on the bed. I stare at it for inspiration. Then I have a thought. I could go to a shop that sells them, and say

I've lost the key. Maybe that's too easy. It is a safe, after all. It's worth a phone call, though.

I Google safe boxes and find a shop. I dial the number. A man answers.

'Sorry to bother you,' I say, 'but I have a safe box and no key. How can I get one, please?'

'What make is it?'

'I don't know. There's nothing on it to tell me.'

'I'd need to see it. Is it your box?'

'Um, it was with my parents' things when we cleared their house. We've never found the key and don't have a clue what's in it.'

'That's difficult because you need to show proof of ownership. You could just take it to a locksmith, I suppose, but they would probably have to drill it.'

'Ok, thanks.'

I get a paper clip and start fiddling with the lock just as Zak appears at the bedroom door.

'You know what curiosity did, don't you?' he grins.

'I don't like being beaten.'

'Neither do I, but this thing's bomb proof. There might be a way of forcing it open, or drilling it, but we don't want Jack to know. We need to be able to do it without leaving a mark.'

'I'll bet Jack expects you to open it!'

Zak laughs. 'Yeah, you're probably right. We'd better not let him down then, had we?'

He starts to take a serious look at the lock. Then he takes two paper clips, opens them up, and pushes one into the lock. He asks me to hold that one still while he rattles the other one about. Nothing.

We try again. According to the internet, it's possible to open this type of lock with paper clips. We're daft enough to try it as demonstrated in a video and bingo! It actually works! Some safe!

Zak cautiously opens the lid as though it might explode. Well, you never know.

After all that, there's just a piece of paper. Bit like our suitcase of disappearing cash in France. So many disappointments!

I pick it up. It's a map.

'Why would you put a map in a safe?' asks a disgruntled Zak. 'He could have brought that home in his pocket!'

I look closer. 'It's got an "x" on it, as in "x" marks the spot.'

'What's this? Treasure bloody Island? Let me see.'

I hand it to him and flop on the bed, exhausted.

'Hellooo, is anybody home?'

It's Cassie.

'Just coming!' I shout. So, normal life is resumed. I go down, and we have a cup of tea and a natter in the kitchen.

She suddenly looks serious. 'Verity, can I ask you something...promise not to be mad?'

'Go on.'

'Well, you did tell me that you were going to, well, get rid of Chester.

'And then he turns up dead near here, not where he lives in London.

96

'And Joyce at number 17 saw you and Zak having a row with a man on your doorstep a while ago…'

I say nothing. She looks at me.

'I'm still waiting for the question,' I say, while frantically trying to think what to say next.

I'm saved by Zak coming into the room, still clutching the map.

'Hi, Cass,' he says and gives her a brief air kiss. 'What's new?'

'The police want to speak to you,' she says.

'So I gather.'

'It's a scream really; they think you look like the person in the Covent Garden video.'

'I wish,' says Zak. 'I'd be rich.'

'You'll have to prove where you were that day,' Cassie continues. 'They will come back.'

'I've no doubt. I'll have to try to remember.'

I decide to be brazen.

'Cassie thinks I murdered Chester.'

Cassie is horrified. 'I didn't exactly say that, Verity... I was just…'

'I'm sure Cassie doesn't think that,' says Zak, and looking at Cassie, 'Why would you?'

'Well, after what he did to Melody… I know how upset you were…I wouldn't blame you.'

'You women have too much imagination,' says Zak. 'Now let's have something to eat. I'm starving.'

Chapter Ten

Zak needs an alibi for his trip to Covent Garden. He trusts his ex-army buddies more than anyone else and decides to see his old pal Angus.

Angus was always a live wire and great fun to be with. They had been through a lot together, and they had always had each other's backs.

Angus lives alone now, not far from here in a remote country cottage on farmland.

Zak wants to do this on his own, so I wish him luck, and off he goes.

I get a cup of coffee and sit down to look at the map.

It's a map of East Hertfordshire, not a million miles from here. The cross, with a circle around it, has been drawn in a village called Cottered in a field behind a village hall.

I think Jack's having a lend of us, as my mother would say. He knows Zak will open the box, and now wants us to be running around the countryside digging up fields!

There's a knock at the door.

'Come in, Cassie,' I call.

Another knock. I go to the door, and a man and a woman are standing there, both wearing lanyards with their police ID.

The man speaks. 'I'm Sergeant Hill, and this is DC Jordan. Is Zak Bently here?'

'No, I'm afraid not.'

'When will he be back?'

'I'm not sure, why?'

'We'd like a word. Are you Verity Brown?'

'Yes.'

'May we come in?'

'Well, Zak's not here.'

'We'd like a word with you,' say the DC.

They come into the sitting room, all the time looking around. The map is on the coffee table, and the woman has a look at it. Damn.

We all sit.

'Mrs Brown, or may I call you Verity?' he asks.

'Verity's fine.'

'Could you please tell us where you were on March 21st?'

'I have no idea off hand,' I say.

'The car in the drive is registered to you, isn't it?'

'Yes.'

'That car was in Covent Garden on that date.'

'Ok, yes, I sometimes go into London to shop.'

'On March 21st, did you take your partner, Zak, with you?'

'He sometimes comes with me, but I can't remember that particular day.'

'Let me jog your memory. It was the day that the HSBC bank was robbed in Covent Garden.'

At that moment, Zak walks in as cool as a cucumber. He walks across to me and kisses me on the forehead.

'What's all this, then?'

The officers introduce themselves.

I say, 'They want to know if you came with me when I went shopping in London on March 21st. I can't say I remember. Sometimes you do, sometimes you don't.'

As brazen as anything, Zak says, 'Yes, I remember that day because there was a bank robbery. I saw it on the news at my mate's house. Don't you remember, I joked about it with you, asking what you'd done with the money?'

'So, where were you that day, sir?' asks the woman.

'I was at my friend's house. He wanted me to help him put up some shelves; he's useless at DIY.'

'And this friend is?'

'Angus Warburton.'

'Address?'

'Crocus Cottage, Becket's Farm, Rushden. Why all the questions?'

'Routine, sir. A man fitting your description was seen on CCTV leaving the bank.'

'I wish it had been me! I could use the money,' Zak laughed.

'That's what they all say. You're the tenth look alike we've seen. Well, that's all for now, thank you. We'll see ourselves out.'

As they leave, I put my fingers to my lips to keep Zak quiet until I check for bugs. Well, they do bug people!

To be certain, we go to the bedroom to talk.

'They'll go straight round to talk to Angus,' I say.

'No worries, he's solid.'

'But they know I was in Covent Garden!'

'You're allowed to go shopping.'

'That woman had a look at the map. It was on the coffee table.'

He laughs and grabs me, 'Ah, well, my hearty, let's hope she finds the treasure for us,' he says in a mock pirate's voice as he swings me onto the bed.

We text Jack and arrange to return the box to him in London in three days' time.

Even though I think he's having a laugh with us, I'm still just a little bit curious about the map.

'What I don't get,' I say to Zak over dinner, 'is why he would give us the money to get home, and then give us another grand for returning the box to him. It doesn't make sense.'

'Even if the map is important,' he continues, 'he could have travelled with it without a problem. Why would he need to put it in a heavy safe box?'

'Maybe there's something else hidden away in the box?'

'Nah, it's solid metal.'

'Just for fun, shall we go and see what's there? It'll be a drive out into the countryside.'

'Yeah, Jack will probably be sitting there like a gnome waiting for us to arrive.'

There's more silly, giggly banter about Jack and his map, but we can't resist going to have a look at the place that is marked with a cross.

We're just about to leave the next morning when a police car pulls up outside. It's the same two officers.

'Hello again,' says Zak, cool as ever.

We all go into the sitting room and sit down.

'Just a few more questions,' says the DS. 'Verity, I'm sorry to bring this up, but you sadly lost your daughter not so long ago?'

Another stab in my heart. 'Yes.'

'And she had been in an abusive relationship with her husband, Chester Robinson?'

'Yes.'

'Did you blame him for her death?'

I see red. 'Of course, I bloody did! She was black and blue and half-starved. He should have been behind bars if you lot had done your job…'

Zak jumps in, 'Where is this leading? You can see you're upsetting her.'

'I'm sure you will have heard that Chester Robinson has been murdered. He had on him money from the Covent Garden bank robbery and was found not far from here.

'We know Verity was in Covent Garden that day, and a man looking like you, sir, was also seen.

'It would appear that Verity had a motive to want to get rid of Chester Robinson.'

Zak stands, 'I hope you're not suggesting…'

'Please sit down, sir, we're not suggesting anything. Just pointing out the facts.'

'Right,' says Zak. 'For a start, you know where I was on that day. I'm sure you will have spoken to Angus. And yes, of course, Verity was angry that her daughter was murdered by that vile creature, but that doesn't make her a murderer. I'm sure there are hundreds of people who had a motive to kill him. Now please go.'

They get up and leave.

I'm in bits, but Zak insists we have a cup of tea and then carry on as normal.

'Don't get upset, it was just a fishing trip,' he says.

An hour later, we're in the picturesque village of Cottered with thatched cottages, one gourmet pub, no shops. We easily find the village hall and park.

The cross on the map is just behind the village hall in a field. There's no gate, so it's easily accessible. Jack is not sitting there waiting for us like a gnome.

The field has been ploughed, so there's no way of knowing if the earth has been disturbed by anyone else. We roughly locate the spot and wander around, kicking clumps of earth here and there but finding nothing obvious.

Should we have brought a spade? Maybe, but we could have been digging for weeks.

We're about to leave when we see a group of children watching us. Unusual to see young children without adults these days, but I suppose in the country, it's different. I give them a smile. One little boy beams back, and I think of my grandson and want to weep.

A girl of about eight, with long red curls, climbs onto the two-bar fence.

'Are you going to dig it up again?' she asks.

'Dig what up again?' says Zak.

'Shush, it's a secret,' says a boy of about the same age.

'It's ok,' I smile. 'You can tell us.'

'The man said it's a secret, and if we tell anybody, we'll be in a lot of trouble,' says little miss redhead.

'Which man?' asks Zak.

The children look at each other and run off.

We wander about, kicking at the soil, looking for anything that isn't mud. Then we go across the road to the pub and have a drink in the garden.

'Now what?' I want to know.

'I've no idea. There must have been something buried there for the kids to know about it. But it might have been moved once the guy, or Jack if it was him, knew that the kids had seen him.'

'Without knowing the exact spot, it would be a waste of time digging,' I say, stating the bleedin' obvious.

As we speak, a police van passes the pub and goes to the back of the village hall.

'You don't suppose…' I start.

'You said that the policewoman saw the map in your house?'

'Yes, she did. And they're going to see our car parked there!'

'No law against it.'

'Good job we hadn't started digging.'

'If we hang about, they might dig it up for us.'

'Jack might not appreciate that.'

An hour later we walk back to the car, and the police have cordoned off the area of the field and erected a kind of tent, the type they use when they find dead bodies.

We are far enough away for them not to notice us as we get into the car.

'Oh my God, I hope it's not a body. I never thought of that. I was thinking guns or valuables.'

'Me too,' said Zak.

'You've known Jack for years. What do you reckon?'

'I reckon we keep out of it and take the box back to him unopened.'

When we get back to the house, the police are waiting in an unmarked car, but we recognise them. We're tempted to keep on going, but they've seen us.

We all settle in the sitting room.

The man speaks. 'There's been an interesting development,' he says, watching us both closely.

'Oh yes?' says Zak, as he picks at the crisps that we'd left on the coffee table.

'Yes. Most of the money from the bank robbery in Covent Garden has turned up in France.'

'Wow,' says Zak. 'I wonder how it got over there.'

'Yes, we were wondering that,' says the woman. 'You were in France recently, weren't you?'

'Yep, little road trip. We all need a break.'

'We do indeed,' says the man. 'You were quite the hero, I understand.'

'Well, not really,' says Zak modestly.

'But the problem is that your heroic deed put you in the area where the money was discovered.'

'Wish I'd known that at the time,' says Zak, still as laid back as ever.

'Yeah,' I say, trying to match the mood, 'We could have stayed in five-star hotels.' I'm ignored.

The man continues, 'You can see our problem. You, Verity, were in Covent Garden on the day of the robbery, and a man who looks like you, Zak, was caught on CCTV, although you say you were at a friend's house.

'Then you take a trip to France, and lo and behold, the money turns up there.

'Some of the cash is also found on the body of your son-in-law, Verity, who was found not a million miles from here.' He waits for a response. There is none.

I wait for a smartarse comment from Zak, but he just shrugs and eats more crisps.

'Maybe we should talk about this down at the station,' says the cop.

'Are you arresting us?' I ask.

'Do you want me to?'

Zak stops munching. 'Look, we've done nothing wrong. If you're going to arrest us, do it. If not, I would appreciate it if you would leave now, and stop harassing us.'

The couple get up to leave.

'I don't believe in coincidences,' says the man. 'We'll be in touch.'

When they've gone, we go for a walk in the woods so that we can talk, just in case they left a bug in the house. We sit on our usual log.

'I'm getting scared,' I mutter.

'I've told you they're just fishing. If they had evidence, they would arrest us. You must keep your nerve.'

'I wonder how they got the money in France?'

'Yes, I was wondering that. The guy must have got nicked or left the money somewhere stupid.'

107

'Like in his car,' I couldn't resist it. 'If he was nicked, he could tell them about the car he got it from.'

'I doubt if he would have taken the number.'

'Maybe not, but he would probably have noticed the make and model.'

'Millions of them.'

'I suppose so, but the circumstantial evidence is all building up.'

'It's not proof. We're respectable citizens with no criminal record, and I'm a bloody hero!'

He laughs as he grabs me for a kiss. He's *my* hero.

'Respectable heroes don't go around robbing banks and murdering people,' he grins.

'I should jolly well hope not!' comes a male voice out of nowhere.

My neighbour, Arthur, appears with his black Labrador, Ben.

We both jump guiltily. How long has he been there?

'I saw the police at your house. You haven't been robbing banks and murdering people again have you, Verity?' he laughs.

'Yes, but don't tell anybody,' I giggle nervously.

Zak jumps in. 'They came for a statement. We witnessed a car crash.'

'Oh, how awful, not a bad one, I hope?'

'No, but the driver was uninsured.'

'Terrible. These days people have no respect for the law.'

We nod in unison. I don't know how Zak does it.

'Well, I'd better make tracks and take this monster for his walk. Oh, by the way, did you manage to get rid of that awful man who was making a scene on your doorstep? I suppose it was a few weeks ago now, but I was in two minds about whether to come over and help you, but then I saw you take him inside, so I'm sure you had everything under control.' My heart starts to race. As usual, Zak to the rescue.

'Thanks, yes, he was drunk. Slept it off. No problem.'

'Ah, that's good. You do meet them, don't you! I'll see you, then.'

'Yes, bye.'

Another nail in our coffin. Zak is unperturbed, and we stroll home hand in hand.

Today we're meeting Jack in London. We go on the train as parking is a nightmare. Zak carries the mystery box in his backpack. It really weighs him down.

We get off at Kings Cross and meet Jack in a nearby bar. He's looking very pleased with himself or maybe just pleased to see us.

He hugs us both and buys our drinks. There is definitely a bond between the two men.

We make small talk for a while, and then Zak removes the box from his backpack and puts it on the table. He just looks at Jack.

'You kept it safe then, well done, Sarge,' says Jack. 'Did you open it?'

'You're kidding; it's like Fort Knox.'

'So, you tried, then?'

'Of course,' grinned Zak.

'The Sarge I knew wouldn't let this thing beat him. You opened it, didn't you?'

'Give me the grand, and I'll tell you.'

Jack reaches into his inside pocket and passes an envelope to me.

'Here, Verity, you have it. He doesn't deserve it; he's been naughty.'

'Ok,' I say, 'spill the beans. What's it all about?'

Jack sips at his beer. 'You want the truth?'

'No, I want you to lie to us,' says Zak.

'Ok, you might not like it, but this is the truth. Zak, when we were on the front line you saved my neck more than once. When we bumped into each other in Germany, you were down on your luck and pretty much stranded. I was getting a flight and didn't want to lug this heavy box around with me, so it made sense for you to take it in the car, and it gave me a chance to help you out without you seeing it as charity.'

Zak picks up the envelope. 'So, this is bloody charity, then?'

'Let me finish, Sarge. No, it's not. But if it helps you out...you'd do the same for me.'

I jump in. 'We saw the map. What was that about?'

'Ah, the map. Bet you couldn't resist going to X marks the spot! It's not far from you, is it.'

'We did,' says Zak, 'But when we got there the police were digging it up.'

The colour drained from Jack's face.

110

'Are you serious?'

'Totally.'

With that, Jack picks up the box and leaves. Zak calls after him, but he's gone.

Chapter Eleven

We have no idea what's going on but decide to stay in town and spend some of the cash on a decent meal.

As Zak puts down his knife and fork, he grins, 'Thanks, Jack, good bit of grub.'

'What on earth had he buried?' I ask.

'No idea. The bloke's a nutter. But he's a good mate. We'll probably find out sooner or later.'

'I hope he's not in trouble.'

'Trouble's his middle name. Don't worry about Jack. He's fireproof!'

That was yesterday. Zak's gone to have a catch up with his friend Angus, and I can't forget about the police digging up the field. It seems obvious that Jack wanted us to find whatever it was. He knew Zak would open the box and find the map.

I could kick myself for leaving it where the policewoman could see it.

I decide to take a drive out to Cottered and see if local people are talking about it.

I go to the pub and pretend I am expecting to meet someone. I get chatting to the barman, a middle-aged guy with a dour demeanour. Well, I chat, he says very little.

I mention that I saw the police across the road behind the village hall the other day, and he says that he's too busy to see what's going on outside. He doesn't look busy to me, but I leave and go to the field.

The children are there again. A new gate has been fitted, and they're sitting on it.

I give them my best smile. 'Hi, again. Nice to see you.' No reply. They just stare at me.

'I saw the police were here the other day. Did you see them?'

This seems to animate them. A boy of about nine says, 'Yes, we all saw them. They put up a tent.'

A little girl in a red dress piped up, 'I thought they were camping like we do in the Brownies.'

The boy looked up to heaven. 'No, silly, they were digging something up.'

'Do you know what they dug up?' I ask, holding my breath.

'It was a big box,' said the boy, puffing out his chest with importance. 'They opened it, and I couldn't see what was in it because they wouldn't let us get close, but a piece of paper flew out of it in the wind, and they didn't see it. It flew near us. The wind nearly knocked the tent over.'

'Yes, and a branch fell off that tree,' said another boy.

'Did you see what was on the piece of paper?' I ask.

The boy reached into his trouser pocket and pulled out a crumpled note.

'It's just a bit of rubbish. Don't make sense.'

'May I see it?' I ask gently.

The boy hands it to me. It's muddy and screwed up, but it reads,

Well done, Sarge, you never disappoint me. This is your share from Afghanistan.

I thought I'd make you work for it. I know how you like a challenge! J.

The boy lets me keep the note, and I drive home deep in thought. Zak's share of what?

Whatever it was, the police had it now. But thank goodness they didn't have the note, although no names were mentioned.

Zak arrives home in a chirpy mood. He and Angus always have a laugh together, and a pint or six.

We're eating an early dinner of lasagna and salad when I decide to tell him my news.

'I went back to Cottered today,' I begin.

'Oh yeah?' he chews absently.

'Yes. I went to the X marks the spot place.'

'Why would you do that?'

'To see if anyone knew what had been dug up.'

'I thought we were going to leave that alone.'

'The police dug up a box, and this note was in it.'

Zak stops eating. 'How the hell did you get the note that was in it?'

'The wind caught it as they opened the box and some kids picked it up. The police didn't notice it, apparently.'

'What does it say?'

'Here, read it for yourself.'

Zak reads it carefully, puts it down and starts pacing about the room.

'Your share of what?' I ask.

'The daft bugger playing games. Now nobody gets it.'

'Gets what?'

There's a knock on the door. Cassie really does pick her moments. Zak says hi to her, and then leaves, just saying he's going out for a while.

'Was it something I said?' laughs Cassie as she makes herself at home at the kitchen table.

'He probably thinks we want to have a girly chat,' I smile, cursing her timing.

Cassie is beaming. 'Guess what!' she says, wriggling with excitement, 'I have a new boyfriend!'

'Wow, you're a dark horse,' I say, putting on the kettle and taking mugs from the cupboard. 'Tell me more.'

'Well,' she says, sounding like a teenager, 'It was strange. I kept bumping into him. Firstly, he helped me with my shopping in Sainsbury's, and then the next day, he was walking past my house as I came out. And yesterday, I parked in the town, and he pulled in beside me.'

'Sounds like a stalker!'

'Oh, you would say that! We had a chat and he asked me out. Said he had wanted to ask me on that day in the supermarket but was too shy.'

'What's he like?'

'Um, well about my age…or in his forties anyway, tall, smiley…'

'Good looking?'

'Not George Clooney, but pleasant. I'm seeing him tonight. We're going for a meal.'

'Cassie, you know nothing about this man. Please be careful. Don't get in his car.'

116

'No, I'll meet him at the restaurant and drive myself home.'

'He'll probably want to come back to yours.'

'On a first date? Not likely!'

'Ok, but ring me if there's a problem.'

'Will do, but, Verity, I really like him, and he seems to have taken a fancy to me.'

I look at her and smile. I do hope this is a new beginning for her, but I'm worried that she'll fall for anyone who shows her some affection.

'What's his name?' I ask, realising that I have been pouring cold water on her dream.

'Scott, his name's Scott,' she grins.

'Try to sneak a picture of him. I'd love to see him,' I say as I watch her scoff yet another chocolate biscuit.

She's gone by the time Zak gets home. She wants time to find something to wear and get ready.

He's very quiet.

'Everything ok, hun?' I ask.

'Yeah.'

'Come on, tell me. We don't keep secrets from each other.'

He joins me at the kitchen table, and I make him a coffee.

'Ok. I haven't been able to contact Jack, but I think I know what he buried.'

'Well?'

'When we were in Afghanistan, the Americans were transporting gold bars from Syria that ISIS had stolen. We helped them out.'

'And helped yourselves.'

'Yes, everyone did. There didn't seem to be any records kept. We only took a few each. There were hundreds of them! When we came home, Jack took charge of them because he was coming back by military aircraft, and he knew all the crew. With everything that's been going on, I wasn't in any hurry to get my share. I was glad he was storing it because I needed to work out what to do with gold bars. Do you melt them down or can you just sell them? I don't know. Now the police have them. Jack is such a loony!'

'You're as bad as each other! Maybe third time lucky. You've nearly been rich twice, so maybe you'll win the lottery!'

He puts his head in his hands, and I can't help feeling sorry for him. He's a lovable rogue, and I'd be lost without him.

I change the subject and tell him about Cassie and Scott, the new love of her life.

He's concerned about the stalking aspect, but I manage to persuade him she's going to be careful.

We go to bed early, both exhausted.

Today I decide that we've had enough drama, and I want to relax. But not much chance of that as Zak is going through his finances and fretting. He had thought that his money worries were over, but now we are both unemployed and broke.

Employers aren't keen on people of our age and especially people who have big gaps in their employment history.

He goes into pacing mode, which drives me nuts. He would have worn a track in the carpet if we had one.

Then he stops and looks at me.

'Jack must have kept some of the gold,' he says.

'Yes, his share.'

'But he lost my share for me, so he should share what's left.'

'Do you think he would?'

'Maybe, if I could track him down. His number's dead.'

'He's probably got a burner. He was spooked by the police getting involved.'

'Angus knows him. I'll see if he knows how to get hold of him.'

He goes off to call him. I look idly at my phone and notice a missed call from Cassie.

Oh no, it was last night. I was dead to the world. There's no message.

I try to call her, but her phone is switched off. I don't want to alarm Zak, so I slip out and go to her flat. No answer.

As I come back in, Zak looks at me.

'Where did you disappear to?'

'I couldn't get hold of Cassie, so I went to her flat.'

'And?'

'She's not there.'

'Probably shopping.'

'Zak, I had a missed call from her late last night.'

'She was probably letting you know she was home safely.'

119

'I hope so.'

'Who is this bloke she was seeing?'

'All I know is that he's in his forties and called Scott.'

'Well, that narrows it down.'

'Let's not panic. She's probably fine. I'll keep trying to get her. Did you get hold of Angus?'

'Yes, luckily he's seeing Jack next week, so I'll go with him.'

'That's good. Fingers crossed then.'

It's 9pm, and I'm getting worried about Cassie. Her phone is still switched off, and she's not answering her door. Zak is watching football on tv.

'Zak, do you have a key to Cassie's place?'

'Uh?'

'Do you have a key to Cassie's place?'

'Fucking ref needs to go to Specsavers, what an idiot!'

'Zak!'

'What...I'm in the middle of a match.'

I so want to switch off the tv, but I control myself.

'Your sister is still missing.'

'Uh?'

'Cassie is missing! Give me her key!'

Mercifully, the ads come on.

'She still not back?' says Zak, finally giving me half his attention.

'I think we should go to her flat. Where's her key?'

He gets up and goes to the bookshelf where a bunch of keys sits on a small tray. He takes one off and hands it to me.

'You want me to go on my own?'

'Verity, I'm trying to watch this match!'

'Don't you care about your sister?'

'She's a grown-up. Stop nursemaiding her. She's probably gone for a dirty weekend with this Scott bloke.'

'Or maybe he's murdered her!'

'In that case, there's no rush, is there.'

'Zak!'

'Ok, ok,' he sighs. 'Come on, then.'

He's still looking back at the screen as we walk out of the door.

Cassie's flat is spotless as ever, but there's no sign of her. Her bed is made. There's mail on the hall floor. The shower is dry.

I try her phone again. Still switched off. She's been gone for over 24 hours now.

I leave her a note to call us, and we go home.

'Should we call the police?' I ask Zak.

'They would just say she's an adult. She doesn't have to tell us where she's going.'

'Ok, but she was meeting a guy who'd been stalking her. Surely that makes a difference.'

'You said he wasn't stalking her!'

'Ok, he kept bumping into her…'

'Well, they're not going to do anything tonight. If she's not back in the morning, we'll give them a ring. But jeez, that's the last thing we need, to be talking to coppers. They already think we're involved in Chester's death; now they'll probably think I've bumped my sister off!'

In the morning, we are sleepily eating our toast and drinking our first coffee of the day when the house phone rings. I jump up to answer it.

'That'll be her,' I say hopefully.

It's a male voice. 'Put Zak on.'

I turn to Zak and put on the speakerphone. 'It's a rude person for you.'

He looks puzzled and takes the phone.

'Hello?'

'Is that Zak?'

'Who wants to know?'

'You have something of mine, and I want it back.'

'Like what?'

'Like the proceeds of a lavender deal.'

'What?'

'You know what I'm talking about, smartarse.'

'I haven't a clue.'

'Then you'd better start remembering, or your sister won't be home anytime soon.'

'Are you saying you have Cassie?'

'You're quick.'

'Let me speak to her.'

'No. You can have her back when you return what's mine.'

'I don't have it. I swear.'

The caller hangs up.

'Shit, shit, shit!' Zak curses.

I feel a bit odd and have to sit down. Cassie's been kidnapped by those vile men.

Poor innocent Cassie.

'How the hell did they trace me?' Zak is pacing.

'We'll have to call the police now!' I stutter.

'No... no... let me think... they're the mob from the industrial unit. I bet she's there. They might have traced me, but they may not know that we know about the unit. The bug's still there, let's go and listen!'

My Zak is a genius!

Forty-five minutes later, we are parked on the road outside the industrial estate. We have an earpiece each. Not a sound. Maybe the battery's dead.

There are two cars parked outside the unit. Then a voice. It's the boss, the voice we heard on the phone.

'I'm going to get a paper.'

'Can you get some beers?' It's Tony, the thug.

'Too early for boozing. Drink some coffee.'

'Can you get some fags?'

'Must you? Ok.'

Zak and I look at each other. This is fascinating stuff! Still, at least we'll get a look at one of them. I get my phone ready to take a picture.

The boss saunters out of the yard, looking deep in thought. He is late forties, six feet tall, with short grey hair and a military bearing.

Zak ducks down, and I pretend to be on my phone but am taking pictures of him. He doesn't look our way but walks past towards a small parade of shops. I get some good clear shots.

We continue to listen in. There are footsteps, a kettle being filled.

Zak looks crestfallen. 'Don't think she's there.'

'What are they doing there?' I ask. 'They're obviously bored and just killing time.'

'I'm going in!'

'No, Zak! It could be a trap. They might be waiting for you!'

'There's only one of them in there at the moment. I can handle him.'

'You can't know that. What about an anonymous phone call to the police to say Cassie is being held in there?'

'I suppose at least we'd find out.'

I look up to see if the boss is returning yet. I can't believe my eyes.

'Is that? No, it can't be…' Zak follows my gaze.

'What is she doing?' He reaches for the car door handle.

'No, wait,' I pull him back.

We watch as Cassie walks arm in arm with 'the boss', laughing and looking lovingly at him.

'At least we know she's ok,' I say.

This time I can't stop Zak. He gets out of the car and confronts the couple as they get nearer.

Cassie throws her arms around him. 'What a surprise! What are you doing here? I tried to phone you but…'

'But she lost her phone,' says the boss.

'This is Scott. I told you about him. Scott, this is my brother, Zak.'

Zak has that look in his eyes. I can hardly bear to look.

124

Chapter Twelve

For a second, there is silence while the two men stare at each other. Both are ex-military men, an even match. I get out of the car in the hope of preventing violence, but I'm too late.

Zak lunges at 'Scott' and takes him down. Cassie starts screaming, and people start appearing from the industrial units and nearby houses.

Zak shouts at Cassie, 'Get in the car!'

'No, what are you doing to Scott? Stop that!'

I chime in, 'Cassie, get in the car. We'll explain...you're in danger!'

Zak shouts, 'DO IT NOW!'

Cassie gets into the car with me, and we lock the doors.

Zak is kneeling on 'Scott's' chest and is pushing his face to one side on the pavement.

'You EVER come near me or my family again, you lowlife, and I'll...'

Suddenly, and without warning, Scott pushes Zak off and is in control. His sidekick Tony has come running from the unit, and the two of them start laying punches into Zak.

Zak fights back like a tiger, but it's two against one. I have to help him.

I unlock the doors, pick up the baseball bat that Zak keeps in the car, and run at them.

My heart is pumping so hard that I can feel it in my mouth. If I get this wrong, I could hit Zak.

They hardly notice me. I swing the bat as hard as I can and hit Tony in the face. He rounds on me, and there's blood everywhere. I've splattered his nose.

I hear a police siren in the distance, and Tony runs for the unit, followed by a staggering Scott.

I get Zak back into the car as quickly as possible and drive off.

Zak has taken quite a beating but insists he's okay.

When we get home, we're all in a state of shock. Zak goes to take a shower and lie down.

I ask Cassie what she was playing at.

'Well, you know I had a date with Scott, and he was really nice. He asked me to stay with him for the weekend, and I thought, what the heck, I'm not doing anything else, and I'm not getting any younger. I tried to phone you, but you didn't answer. Then I lost my phone… what was that all about today?'

'Your so-called Scott is a villain. Zak knows him, and he's a really bad guy. He rang Zak and said he'd kidnapped you!'

'What? Why would he do that?'

'To get money out of Zak. That's what he does. You had a lucky escape thanks to your brother.'

'But how did you know where I was?'

'You'll have to ask Zak that. Now go home and have a rest, and block that vile man from contacting you.'

Once she's gone and Zak's asleep, I get in my car and go back to the scene. My car won't be recognised.

There is nothing to see. The police have gone.

I want to listen in, although I'm probably too late. I put on my earphones.

'I'm off, then,' I think it's Tony, but he's sounding nasal.

'You going to let the wife see you looking like that?'

'I'll tell her I got drunk last night and fell down. She'll believe that. You're not looking so good yourself.'

'I've been worse.'

'Can't let that little shit win.'

'I don't intend to.'

'See ya, then.'

'Yep.'

It's not over. I'll have to tell Zak. Maybe we should move.

As I drive home, I think of all the options.

Sell up and move...probably the best option, but it takes time, and wherever we go, we could be tracked down.

Go straight away and let out the house. But where to?

Blow up the unit with them in it. The evil brain slipped in there again for a minute.

Change our identities and go abroad.

Stay where we are and wait to see what happens, but we'd be nervous wrecks...well, I would be.

Zak is watching TV when I get back. He looks awful.

'Don't go bloody disappearing without telling me!' he snaps.

'Sorry, sweetheart. You were asleep.'

'Where were you?'

I plonk myself down beside him.

'I went to the unit to listen in.'

'Are you mad?'

'No, listen to me. We need to know what they're going to do next.'

'Did they see you?'

'No, of course not. I took my car.'

'Well?'

'They're not going to leave it at that.'

'Of course they're not, they think I've got their stash of money.'

'So, what can we do? We can't stay here waiting for them to crash in.'

'They won't do anything straight away. They need to plan their tactics.

'I'm seeing Angus and Jack tomorrow. We'll think of something.'

'You going to tell them the whole story?'

'A version of it. I'd trust both of them with my life and have done in the past.'

'I'm coming with you.'

'Verity, this is a bloke thing.'

'Bloke thing be damned! I'm just as involved in all this as you are. I'm not going to sit here on my own while you discuss our futures with your mates.'

'They won't like it.'

'Why not?'

'Well...'

'I'm a woman!'

'If you like.'

'Because I haven't got a dick, I'm what? Not capable of understanding? Likely to cry? What?'

'Ok come, if you feel that strongly about it.'
'I will.'
'Okay.'
'Okay.'

Happily, Zak is in a better mood the next day when we meet up with Angus and Jack in a bar in London. Angus looks surprised to see me, and Jack looks surprised to see both of us.

Once the drinks are in, we get down to business.

'I've been trying to contact you, Jack,' says Zak.

'Yeah, sorry, mate. I've been lying low a bit...'

Angus jumps in. 'Yes, you've all got your problems at the moment. What happened to you, Zak? You look like you've taken a pasting?'

'You should see the other guy,' I quip, maybe predictably because nobody laughs.

To my surprise, Zak tells them the whole story, all of it. They both knew bits, but now they know everything. I feel exposed and look around to make sure nobody is within earshot.

'Blimey,' says Angus. 'This is a bit heavy, even for me.'

Zak hits back, 'You've done worse, mate.'

'Maybe in a war zone.'

Jack is fidgety. 'What do you want from me, guys? I can't stop long.'

Zak's getting irritated. 'Somewhere important to go?' Jack looks into his drink.

I decide to speak up. 'Jack, you lost Zak's gold by playing games with us. Now the police have it. We've lost everything. We'd like you to share your gold with us.'

'It's only fair,' says Zak.

Jack looks at Angus who picks at his nails.

Jack looks at me. 'How did the police know how to find it?'

'Who knows!' says Zak. 'Maybe you were seen.'

'Ok, look, as you know, we had four bars. I buried your two. I'll let you have one of mine.'

'Thanks, mate.'

'You're welcome. Now I must go.'

'Now hang on, when do I get this bar?'

Angus is getting suspicious of Jack. 'I think we should go and get it now while we're all together.'

Zak and I agree. Jack is not happy. 'It's not at my place…'

'So, where is it?' I ask.

'It's in a safety deposit box at the bank. We can't all troop in there. Anyway, the banks close in a minute…'

'Which bank?' asks Zak.

Jack has to admit defeat, and as there is twenty minutes before the banks close, we rush to Santander which is two streets away.

We all go in, but only Jack is allowed to go into the strong room. He comes out carrying a heavy canvas bag. As we leave the bank, he passes the bag to Zak.

'Be lucky,' he grins and walks off in the opposite direction.

Once home, we study the solid gold bar. It's so beautiful. We have no idea of its value, so we go online and discover we're talking about £50k.

'That'll do nicely,' says Zak as he swings me around the room. I wish he wouldn't do that!

All we have to do now is somehow change it into money without arousing suspicions or the tax man! Zak's been researching it and knows what to do. He has a friend of a friend. I leave him to it, and he goes out.

It's the first time I've had time to think for a while, and I suddenly think of my darling daughter, and I feel I've been punched in the stomach. Huge sobs overtake me, and I wail like a banshee. My pain is as raw as it was the day she died. I think of her little boy, and the pain is unbearable. I sob until I'm exhausted.

I look in the mirror. Where is Verity Brown, respectable middle-aged housewife? Widow of a businessman? Ex charity shop manager? Who is this red-eyed, drawn replacement?

The man who caused my pain is dead, and I'm glad of that and not ashamed of the thought. But my anger and despair have set me on a road of no return. A road I would never have dreamed of taking.

I just want things to go back to the way they were. Normal, everyday stuff. I don't want to live in fear of criminals and the police.

But nothing I do can change any of that now. And even worse, I have turned the kind, adorable Zak into a killer and a criminal. Or maybe he already was one, I'm not sure.

I've even involved Cassie, my best friend. And none of it has brought my daughter back.

I feel a deep sadness in the pit of my stomach and an overwhelming feeling of exhaustion and despair. What will the future hold? Years of imprisonment? Being attacked by a gang?

I just can't see a future. I sink into a fitful sleep on the sofa.

I'm woken by the front door slamming. Zak walks in and switches on the light.

'Why are you sitting in the dark...oh sorry, honey, were you sleeping?' He looks very pleased with himself. 'It's a lot easier than you'd think,' he says, taking wads of £20 notes from a canvas bag and placing them on the coffee table. I sit and look at it.

'What's up? Have you been crying?' he asks, looking concerned.

'Just thinking of my little girl,' I say, trying to pull myself together.

'These things take time,' he says, 'but it'll get easier. At least we don't have any money worries now.'

'No,' I say, flatly.

'This is legit money now. We can have a proper holiday. I'll try not to leave it in the car!'

He gives me a big grin, and I fall into his arms and cry all over again.

A few days later, I'm feeling a lot brighter as we board a plane for Alicante. Maybe we *can* lead a normal life. Maybe in time we will just be another couple like any other.

The flight is uneventful, and it's exciting to arrive in sunny Spain. We hire a car and drive for an hour north along the coast to Calpe where we've booked a villa.

It's a beautiful place, whitewashed walls with red bougainvillea everywhere. There are lemon and orange trees and a large sparkling pool in the back garden, which has a perfect view of the sea and the Calpe rock by the harbour.

We sit in the garden on the soft loungers and relax for the first time in months. We don't speak. We don't need to. Bliss.

Later we shower and change and go for a stroll to the seafront, looking for a place to have dinner.

We find a lovely restaurant right on the beach. The sun's still shining, and the views across the bay are magnificent. Zak looks at me with love in his eyes. It's as if we're different people here somehow.

'Why don't we stay here?' I say, as our tapas is served.

'Everyone says that when they're on holiday,' laughs Zak.

'No, I mean it. Why don't we move out here?'

'With fifty grand?'

'I could sell my house. That must be worth four hundred grand. We could buy a little bar...'

'Why does everyone who comes to Spain want to buy a bar?'

'Ok, another type of business, then.'

'We don't speak the lingo.'

'We could learn, or we could just cater to the Brits.'

'Is this because you're worried about the police? They can extradite you from here, you know.'

'I know that. Wherever we are, we're taking a chance, but we won't be under their noses here, and the guys from the unit won't know we're here.'

'It is *nice* here…'

We grin broadly at each other, the decision made.

'But we have done some terrible things, haven't we,' I say.

'Have we? Chester murdered your daughter and was halfway to killing his next victim, not to mention depriving a little boy of his mum. I'd say he got justice.

'The lavender bank money was found in France, so will have been returned to the bank, so not much was lost there. Ok, I didn't return it, but maybe I redeemed myself a bit by saving some lives with that gunman episode.

'And the gold bars were taken from ISIS, terrorists! I'm not going to lose any sleep over that.'

'Well, when you put it like that…'

'Stop worrying. Our new life starts here, today.'

And with that, in front of everyone in the restaurant, and to the delight of passers-by, he reaches into his pocket and goes down on one knee.

'Verity Brown. I love the very bones of you. I want to be with you forever. Will you marry me?'

I fling my arms around him and whisper in his ear, 'Only if you stop robbing banks and killing people!'

He laughs as he places a diamond ring on my finger.

'I promise,' he says, 'and you have to promise to stop bugging people.'

We walk back to the villa hand in hand like a pair of teenagers with hope in our hearts and a new spring in our steps.

Chapter Thirteen

If this were a film, we would walk off into the sunset as the credits roll, but this is real life, and now two weeks have passed, and reality has set in.

It isn't as easy as we thought to set up in business here, and in any case, I'll need to sell my house before we can think about it.

We're having coffee at our favourite beachside cafe, watching the world go by when Zak suddenly grabs my arm and yanks me up and drags me behind an ice cream fridge, where we crouch out of sight.

'What?' I start.

'Shhh.'

We watch through a gap in an advertising board as the two detectives who came to my house stroll by.

Once they're out of sight, we rush off in the opposite direction until we get to a busy market where we mingle while we talk.

'How the fuck!?' says Zak.

'I don't know, but we can't go back to the villa.'

'All our stuff's there!'

'The important stuff is in my bag, the passports and money,' I say.

It's unusual to see Zak so rattled, but it was a big shock.

'Maybe they're just on holiday,' I say hopefully, but we both know that's rubbish.

We sit on a bench as the crowds mooch about around us. Zak's looking across the road at a car hire office.

I read his mind. 'We'd have to use our real ID, and they could easily trace the car.'

'Maybe, but it would get us away from here. Give us time to think.'

So here we are an hour later on the mountain road to Valencia.

'We need to get to a country that we can't be extradited from,' says Zak.

'Like where?' I ask.

'Google it,' he says impatiently.

I try to, but there's no signal.

I look at the engagement ring gleaming on my finger and wonder if the dream is over.

The scenery in the mountains is amazing, but we're not seeing it.

Eventually we get to the outskirts of Valencia, and park.

We look up 'places that won't extradite you to the UK'. There are 33 of them. Mainly war zones and countries near Russia that end in 'stan'. Kyrgyzstan, Uzbekistan, Tajikistan...and Belarus.

'Where do you fancy?' says Zak.

'Never heard of them, except Belarus. I think that's near Poland.'

'Or there's China or Japan... or Egypt,' Zak continues.

I'm not sure if he's serious.

Suddenly, I want to go home. Back to normality. Back to my little house in my little street in my little town where nothing happens. I want to turn the clock back so we wouldn't need to be running away.

'Are you ok?' asks Zak.

'I don't want to spend the rest of my life in some country I've never heard of where I don't know the language,' I wail.

He laughs. 'You numpty, neither do I.'

'So, what do we do?'

'We go and eat some tapas and have a beer.'

The shock of seeing the police and then dashing off has left me feeling drained, but Zak seems to be exhilarated by the excitement.

'Right,' he says, as he puts down his beer glass, 'What about this. We go to the station and buy tickets to Madrid. There's bound to be loads of CCTV, so we get on the train but get off at the next station, and get a train to the south of France, say Nice. Then we get a ferry across to Corsica. But we change the way we look as we go and even travel separately.'

'Ok,' I say cautiously, 'and then what?'

'We find ourselves a little flat and live happily ever after.'

'Like we did in Calpe, you mean!'

'Look, wherever we go, the police could eventually find us. And if we're not prepared to live in a freezing offshoot of Russia…'

'How do we change the way we look? We've only got the clothes we stand up in.'

'We can buy a few T-shirts and some hats. I can grow a beard.'

'By this afternoon?' I laugh.

This is how I find myself in sunny Corsica with a lovable lunatic and a carrier bag full of hats and T-shirts.

There is no shortage of holiday lets, so we find a cottage almost on the beach and book it for two weeks to give ourselves time to take stock.

It feels safe here, maybe because it's on an island, which makes no sense at all, but I start to relax. The place is a bit basic but has everything we need except clothes, food and toiletries, so we set off to find some shops.

We are just outside Ajaccio where there are lots of shops, so no problem. We get by with my schoolgirl French and stroll back along the beach hand in hand as if we didn't have a care in the world.

As we arrive back at our cottage loaded down with shopping, a woman approaches us. She looks familiar. She is stunning with long glossy brown hair and curves in all the right places. Zak puts down his shopping and smiles like an idiot.

'Can I help you?' he says in slow, careful English.

The woman smiles, showing her Daz white teeth, and fluttering her eyelashes.

'Oh good, you're English,' she says. 'I'm staying over there,' she looks toward a villa about fifty metres away. 'I'm looking for somewhere to hide for a while.'

'Is someone bothering you?' asks Zak, ready to get into hero rescuer of damsel in distress mode.

'Well, yes. I'm not in danger, but…'

I suddenly remember who she is. She's a big name in one of the TV soaps. I'm not a soap fan, but I've seen her picture in newspapers and magazines.

'You're Georgia Vincent!' I squark, like a star struck teenager.

'Yes,' she purrs, 'That's the problem. There are some fans waiting by my gate, and I can't get into the villa without them seeing me.'

'Are you there on your own?' asks Zak, who has never heard of her.

'Yes, just trying to get some R&R. My husband died six months ago, and this is the first chance I've had to get a break.'

Zak is now the full knight in shining armour.

'Come inside,' he says. 'We'll sort something out.'

As we enter the cottage he whispers, 'Who is she?'

'Soap star,' I hiss.

A bloody glamorous, single, flirty bloody soap star, that's who. And staying right next door. Zak's tongue is on the floor.

'Can I get you a drink?' he asks Georgia, as he rummages in our shopping bags for something to offer her.

'I'd love a cup of tea,' she smiles with her head to one side in a coquettish pose.

Zak runs his fingers through his hair and looks at me. 'Put the kettle on, love,' he says.

I'm thinking, 'put the bloody kettle on yourself', but I say nothing and take the shopping into the kitchen where I put the bloody kettle on.

But I'm not leaving them alone, so I go straight back into the sitting room.

Georgia is sitting on the sofa, her long brown legs crossed, and her silk dress displaying her cleavage. Zak is sitting on the arm of the sofa getting a good view.

'I'm Zak,' he says but doesn't introduce me.

'Georgia,' she smiles.

And I'm the cat's mother, I want to say, but I actually say, 'I'm Verity. How do you like your tea?'

'Black, please, no sugar.'

Well of course she wouldn't take sugar. Look at her!

I go back into the kitchen and make the tea. Two sugars for me, one for Zak.

'Well now,' says the hero of the hour as I return, 'Verity, why don't you go and see if Georgia's fans have left yet, or if they're still hanging around?'

'Oh, would you?' gushes Georgia.

No, I won't, I want to say. Do you think I'm leaving my fiancé alone with you? Why can't he go?

But I hear myself say, 'Okay. Maybe you should come with me, Zak?'

'You'll be fine. It's only up the road,' he says, not even looking at me.

So, like an idiot, I go. I'm raging. Fear will do that to you. The green-eyed monster has taken over. Georgia is a million times prettier and sexier than me, and she's flirting with my man. I doubt there's a man in the world who would turn her down.

I'm soon at the large iron gates of her villa where a group of good-natured people are chatting and laughing.

I could tell them that Georgia's not coming back, and they might leave, but then Zak would be able to spend time with her at the villa uninterrupted. Or I could tell them that she'll be back soon, but then she wouldn't leave our place.

But at least at our place I could keep an eye on things. If Zak walks her home, I might never see him again.

You probably think I'm overreacting. Maybe I am. But I can't lose Zak, not now.

I decide not to say anything to the fans and simply report back that they are still there.

As I return to the cottage, I hear them both laughing. It's like a knife in my stomach.

'Well?' says Zak as I enter.

'They're still there. But they seem pretty harmless.'

'I'm sure that's not the point,' says Zak loftily, 'Georgia doesn't feel up to dealing with these people at the moment.'

'Well how did Georgia get past them to get here?' I ask, equally loftily.

Zak looks at Georgia, 'Is there another entrance?'

'No, I had to climb over a wall,' she whines in a child-like voice. 'This is how I got this,' she says, lifting her dress to show a graze on her thigh.

'We can't have you climbing walls,' says Zak, with his eyes popping out of his head.

I decide to take charge.

'I'm sure my fiancé will be able to shoo the people away, and then I'll walk you home to make sure you're okay,' I smile.

She looks at Zak with doe eyes.

'Oh, do you think you could?' she says.

'Yes, of course…' he stammers, for the moment outwitted. 'Will you come with me, Verity?'

'Oh, you'll be fine. It's only up the road,' I say. 'You don't need me.'

Game, set and match. Off he goes with a sheepish grin.

Georgia pulls her dress back down and looks equally sheepish.

'How long are you here for?' I ask, hoping she's going home tomorrow.

'Only a month, and then it's back to work. You?'

'Not sure yet. We're playing it by ear.'

Maybe *we* will leave tomorrow!

Zak strolls back in as if he's just won a fight at the OK corral. Any minute now, he'll be blowing the smoke from his revolver.

'They're gone,' he says, pulling himself to his full height and smiling at Georgia.

'What did you do?' she asks.

'Oh, just had a word on their ear. They won't be back.'

'Thank you, you're so brave!' she simpers.

'Yes, well done, darling,' I say, kissing him on the cheek. 'I'll walk Georgia home.'

'I'll come with you,' he says.

'It's ok, darling. We want to have a girlie chat, don't we, Georgia? You'd be bored. Why don't you unpack the shopping and relax. I won't be long.'

Zak just stands there, for the first time in his life lost for words.

When we get to the gate of Georgia's villa, I turn to go, but to my surprise, she invites me in. I must admit I'm curious to see how the other half live, so I follow her up the drive and into the spacious living room. She then shows me through to the patio and the enormous infinity pool with views out to sea. There are sun loungers with thick blue cushions with white piping and matching canopies.

Georgia motions for me to sit down and goes back inside. She comes out a few minutes later in a red bikini carrying two glasses of champagne.

She hands me one and sits beside me.

'You don't like me much, do you?' she says. I'm taken aback.

'I hardly know you…' I say.

'But I can tell. I can always tell. Women never like me.'

I want to say, 'Well maybe they would if you didn't flirt with their men,' but instead I say, 'Look, you're a very glamorous woman and a TV star. They're probably jealous.'

'Are you jealous?' she says.

Ok, if she really wants to know… 'Georgia, you were flirting with Zak. He's my fiancé. I didn't appreciate that.'

'He was flirting with me!' she says indignantly. 'Believe me, I know men. You won't have *him* for long!'

Now I'm seething. 'You may not keep your men for long, and I can see why, but I can assure you that Zak and I are solid.'

She stands up and looks straight at me in a menacing way. I stand up, shaking with emotion.

'He wants me,' she laughs. 'He made that clear, you silly naive woman. And I'll have him!'

Well, that's it. I lunge forward and push her into the pool. Then I march out, fighting back the tears of anger that are prickling behind my eyes.

As I hurry down the drive, I'm met by a man with a bunch of flowers who just says, *'Est elle en?'*

I hurry on as tears are beginning to spill, and I'm not sure what he means. He continues up to the villa.

I don't know what to tell Zak. If I tell him that Georgia wants him, he'll be flattered and might take advantage of it. I'll calm myself down and not tell him anything. Maybe I'll say she's going home tomorrow, and hopefully, he'll forget all about her. I might suggest that we move on as well.

Zak can tell that something's wrong, but I just say I'm tired, and we have an early night.

We're woken at 6.15am by sirens. I look out of the window, and there is some sort of a kerfuffle going on at Georgia's place. An ambulance goes up the drive and police arrive. As time goes on, press photographers and TV cameras start to appear.

'What the…' says Zak as he pulls on his shorts and a T-shirt. 'That's Georgia's place. I hope she's alright!' he says as he rushes out of the door.

'She's probably broken a nail,' I think bitchily as I get dressed to follow him.

We can't get near the villa gates. The police are taping the area off.

'What's going on?' I ask anyone who'll listen. People are chattering to each other in French and some in Italian. They ignore me. Zak is being

144

shouted at in French by the gendarmes who are shooing him away.

He comes over to me. 'Wish I could speak French. I can't find out what's going on. You had any joy?' I shake my head.

'Let's go home,' I say. 'We'll find out sooner or later.'

Then a woman's voice from behind me says, 'Do you know what's going on?' I turn and see one of the fans who were at the gate yesterday.

'No, we don't speak French...' I reply.

'Ok, I do,' she smiles. 'I'll see what I can find out.'

She wanders off and talks to a press photographer. She looks shocked and comes back to us with unshed tears in her eyes.

'She's dead. Georgia's dead.'

Zak is animated, 'How, what happened?'

'She was found floating in the pool by the cleaner this morning.'

The woman rushes off in tears.

Zak and I look at each other in horror. Zak puts his arm around me, and we walk back to our cottage.

Chapter Fourteen

It's soon big news. British TV star Georgia Vincent found dead in her swimming pool. Friends say she never used the pool and couldn't swim. She just liked to sunbathe. Police say the body had been in the water for at least 12 hours, maybe more.

'Dear God, she must have died soon after you left her!' says Zak.

She couldn't swim! I pushed her in. She was in a bikini...I assumed...but if she'd been in trouble, that man who arrived as I was leaving would have helped her. Yes, of course he would. Or maybe he killed her?

I suddenly realise Zak is staring at me.

'Are you okay? You're as white as a sheet?'

'Yes, um sorry. It's just such a shock.'

'Was she on her own when you left her? Did she say she was going in the pool?'

'Zak… I pushed her in the pool.'

'What?'

'I pushed her in the pool! She was being foul to me. I didn't know she couldn't swim!'

'What do you mean she was being foul to you?'

'She said you would leave me for her. That she would get you. She said you wouldn't marry me.'

'Don't be ridiculous!'

'That's what she said. She was so smug, and Zak you *were* drooling all over her.'

'So, you killed her!'

147

'NO! She stood up and started to glare at me in a threatening way. I pushed her away from me, and she fell into the pool. I assumed she'd just get out. And, in any case, if she had been in trouble, that man would have helped her out.'

'What man?'

'As I was leaving, a man arrived to see her.'

'Who was he?'

'How should I know? He said something to me in French, but I didn't catch it, and I was upset and rushing away. He did look familiar. Maybe one of the other cast members.'

'Jesus, Verity,' Zak was pacing, 'I was the one who told the fans to leave.'

'What reason did you give?'

'I said Georgia had left the villa, so there was no point in waiting.'

He switches on BBC TV rolling news. Eventually, the story comes up.

Latest: *Cast member Carl Stafford says he went to the villa to see Georgia on the day she died, but there was no answer. As he arrived, a woman ran past him looking upset. Police are appealing for witnesses and checking CCTV in an attempt to try to identify the mystery woman. Earlier, a man had dispersed fans who were waiting at the villa gates saying that Miss Vincent had left the villa and would not be returning. The police would also like to speak with him.*

We don't know whether to laugh or cry. We're just two ordinary people from a small town, and now we're murderers on the run! Did I murder her? Is it murder if you didn't mean to kill someone?

148

'I'll explain,' I say. 'I'll tell them what happened.'

'You won't!' snaps Zak, 'Let's get out of here while we can.'

All we have is a few T-shirts and hats and a bag of food. But we have some money left, so we walk a little way into town and get a cab to the ferry. We have a little while to wait, so we sit on the harbour wall.

Zak starts to relax, and suddenly starts laughing. He puts his arm around me.

'Where would you like to go now, madam? The Savoy or would you like a little jaunt around Nice in my yacht?'

I'm not sure if we should be laughing and fooling around when that woman is dead.

Oh, sod her, she was a piece of work. I can't mourn for somebody like her.

I turn to Zak. 'I think a tour of the south of France in your yacht would be quite acceptable, sir, and I'll dress for the occasion,' I pull a red T-shirt with a smiley face on the front out of the carrier bag and plonk a floppy white sun hat on my head.

Zak grabs the bag and takes a white T-shirt with an anchor on the front and a blue baseball cap and puts them on. I put my T-shirt over my clothes.

He stands up and offers his arm, 'Okay, m'lady, this way, please.'

I take his arm and we walk like a couple of giggling idiots onto the ferry.

We manage to get window seats and settle down for the five-and-a-half-hour journey.

I notice a young woman with a small boy, and I think of my daughter and grandson. He would be about the same age now. He could even be my grandson. How will I ever know what he looks like? The tears start to cascade down my cheeks. Zak is asleep, so I try to compose myself before he wakes.

We have dinner of pizza and salad in the onboard Italian restaurant and arrive in Nice as the sun is going down. It should all be so beautiful, but I feel a sadness deep inside that I can't shake off.

We find a room in a boutique hotel in the old town and fall into bed exhausted.

It's a new day, and the sun is shining as we sit eating our breakfast at a harbourside cafe.

I can't help thinking about the body in the swimming pool. Ok, she was a horrible woman, but she was young and didn't deserve to die. I feel dreadful now that it has sunk in that I may have caused her death. Zak seems deep in thought, too.

'We ought to check on Cassie,' he says, out of the blue. 'We haven't spoken to her in ages. She'll be worried.'

'Yes,' I say, absently.

'And we should change our burner phones just to be on the safe side.'

'Yes.'

'Verity, are you okay?'

'What? Yes, yes, I'm fine,' I force a smile.

'Verity, what's done is done and can't be undone. Move on.'

'Where to? Where do we go from here?'

'We sell your house and find our very own little nest,' he says, taking my hand in his.

'But where?'

'Anywhere you like.'

'Somewhere where they speak English,' I say, brightening a bit.

'Ok, Canada, USA, New Zealand, Australia?'

'They're all so far away. I don't suppose you can just get on a plane and emigrate, just like that!'

'Where there's a will, there's a way,' he grins, as positive as ever. 'I'll ring Cassie and see if she'd be able to sort out the house sale, shall I?'

Am I ready to sell my home? My only security in this world? What other option do we have?

'Yes, why not,' I say, trying to sound cheerful.

'Hi, Cassie, it's Zak.'

'Zak! I wish you wouldn't keep disappearing for weeks at a time. Are you ok? I've been trying to contact you, but you keep changing your phone.'

'Sorry, Cass. We're both fine, thanks. I just wanted to ask you…'

'Before you do, I have something to tell you...'

'What now?'

'Aunt Alice died nine months ago.'

'Do we have an Aunt Alice?'

'No, she's dead, but apparently we did. She was actually Dad's second cousin or something.'

'And?'

'Well, her solicitor has been in touch and says that we are the only living relatives they can trace.'

'And?'

'It's good news and bad news, really. She has a house on the Isle of Wight which is apparently amazing, and we're the beneficiaries.'

'Blimey.'

'And the bad news is it's about to fall off a cliff.'

'Bloody typical of our luck. What do you mean exactly?'

'The solicitor said that it's about a hundred yards from a crumbling cliff, but it's estimated that it will be ok for four or five years. It's unsaleable because nobody would be able to get a mortgage on it, but he said it's structurally sound, and perfectly usable for a few years, with a great sea view!'

'How big is it?'

'He sent me the details. It's a mansion! Worth a fortune before the neighbours started to fall into the sea. Six bedrooms, five reception rooms, including what looks like a ballroom! It's fully furnished and has a huge garden.'

'For fuck's sake! I don't believe it.' Zak is beaming. 'How do we split it up if we can't sell it?'

'Zak, if you and Verity want to live in it, please do. My life is here. As long as I can come for holidays! I know Verity was not happy in her house here. Or we could rent it out and share the proceeds.'

'Let me talk to Verity.'

'Of course.'

'Any other news?'

'Isn't that enough for you?' Cassie laughs. 'Yes, actually, there have been a couple of people looking for you. Don't know who they are so don't ask, but I said you were on holiday, and I didn't know where or when you'd be back...basically the truth.'

'Ok, thanks, Cass. We'll talk soon. Don't give anyone this number.'

'Of course not. Bye, hun.'

Zak is grinning from ear to ear. 'There *is* a God!' he says. 'For you, my sweet, a mansion in an English-speaking country, right by the sea!'

I have only heard his side of the conversation, so I want to hear all the details. He explains with great enthusiasm.

'Go back to England? Are you mad?' I splutter.

'It's not exactly England, it's the Isle of Wight. Who would think of looking for us there?'

'It does sound beautiful,' I admit.

He laughs. 'I said, where there's a will, there's a way!'

You might be thinking that this is the sort of thing that only happens in books. And you'd be right. Just when we were desperate for somewhere to stay, an unknown relative pops her clogs and leaves us a mansion by the sea. You couldn't make it up. Well, you could...

So, today we're on a wonderful train journey through France, and then on a couple of ferries to the little English island.

We get a cab from the ferry to the house. The sun is shining brightly, and everything looks idyllic. The cab stops outside the house, and we can hardly believe our eyes. It's a Georgian mansion with a long gravel drive and manicured gardens.

A solicitor is there to meet us. There are papers to sign and formalities. He has the keys, so we go inside.

There are high ceilings with covings and cornices and large windows giving spectacular sea views. The furniture is covered in sheets. The kitchen is dated but usable, and there is a wood panelled dining room with crystal chandeliers.

Then we wander into a huge room which the solicitor had described as the ballroom. It's hard to see how it could be anything else. Aunt Alice must have been a sociable soul!

We all sit at the dining table to sign the paperwork. Good job we have our passports as ID.

I feel as if I'm in a dream, lurching from crisis to heaven and back again.

It's a fantastic house, but how can we afford to run it? We have a little money left, but it won't last long.

Eventually, the solicitor leaves, wishing us well.

Zak pulls the covers from a large sofa, and lounges on it with a big grin on his face.

'Lady Verity, will you ring for the butler? Yes, call for champagne and maybe a couple of lobsters.'

'Lord Zak, it may be the maid's day off, but I am not your skivvy. Ring your own bell.'

'Very well, my dear. Would you care to eat in the dining room or on the terrace?'

'I think I favour McDonalds, your poshness.'

'Ok, a Mc Lobster it is then.'

As I throw myself onto the sofa next to this madman with a fit of the giggles. We hear a noise from upstairs.

Zak looks startled, but says, 'Worry ye not, fair maiden, that will be Jeeves making the beds.'

Then we hear footsteps on the stairs.

Chapter Fifteen

There is definitely someone coming down the stairs and into the hall. Zak motions for me to hide behind the sofa, and he grabs a poker from the fireplace. He hides behind the door. I dare not raise my head to see the man enter the room, but I hear him.

'Don't hit me!' he yells.

'What are you doing here?' Zak means business.

'I've been looking after the place for Alice.'

'Alice is dead.'

'Yes, I know, but someone needs to keep the place in order until... well, until the new owners arrive.'

I get up from my cowardly hiding place.

Zak says, 'We are the new owners.'

'Oh, I see, well, um, I'll be off then.'

I pipe up, 'Have you been living here?'

'Yes. Alice said I could.'

'So, where will you go?'

'Oh, don't worry about me. I'll find somewhere.'

'What exactly have you been doing...'

'Gardening, keeping the place warm in the winter and aired. Cleaning, that sort of thing.'

Zak asks, 'What's your name?'

'Rip. They call me Rip.'

Zak continues with the third degree, 'Rip, how do you know... did you know Alice?'

'It's a bit of a long story...'

'We're not in a hurry.'

'Well, there used to be a boarding school just down the road. Well, they called it a boarding school, but really it was an orphanage. They've turned it into flats now, but anyway, I was sent there as a boy, and I was miserable. I used to run away at every opportunity, and one day I hid in Alice's garden. She found me and was the kindest person I had ever met. She fought the authorities to take me in, and eventually, I was allowed to come here in the holidays. And when I left school, I came to work for her doing odd jobs and gardening. I loved her like a mother.' Tears start to drip down his handsome, tanned face.

I look at Zak. He is shifting from one foot to the other. Zak doesn't do emotion.

I turn to Rip, 'Do you have any tea in the house, Rip?'

'Yes, yes, would you like some?'

'Yes, please, if you don't mind.'

Rip rushes off to the kitchen.

Zak is nonplussed. 'Tea?'

'I needed to talk to you. Rip knows this place inside out, and we could do with someone to do the garden and odd jobs.'

'And what am I? Chopped liver?'

'You know you hate gardening and DIY.'

'What are you suggesting?'

'We let him stay. We can't just chuck him out onto the street.'

'He's a grown man.'

'Yes, but he could be very useful to us.'

'And who pays his wages?'

156

'Maybe he'd swap board and lodging for help around the place.'

'You fancy him, don't you?' Zak teases.

'Don't be ridiculous.'

'Ok, Lady Chatterley, whatever you say. But if he makes a pass at you…'

'The man's gay!'

'Says who?'

'I have a foolproof gaydar. He's more likely to make a pass at you!'

Rip returns with a tray, a silver teapot, two delicate cups and saucers, milk in a jug and sugar lumps in a silver bowl with tongs. He sets them down on a coffee table.

'Two cups?' I say. 'Aren't you going to join us?'

'I didn't like to presume.'

'Come on, you daft bugger,' says Zak in his usual tactful way. 'We think you should stay. How would you feel about staying and keeping the house in order for us? No wages, I'm afraid, but free accommodation and food.'

Rip looks stunned, and he wells up. 'That would be fantastic, if you're sure.'

'We're sure,' says Zak. 'But only if you get yourself a cup of tea.'

Later we take a closer look at all the rooms. Rip has gone out for the evening.

Naturally, we have to have a look at his room. Everything is clean and neat. Nothing out of place and the bed made. There are posters of Judy Garland and Barbara Streisand on the walls.

157

'Told you!' I crow.

'*I* like Judy Garland and Barbara Streisand,' counters Zak.

'And what about the ballerinas?' I persist.

Zak looks at the framed photographs on the dresser. Then he does an impressive pirouette around the room.

'I like ballet too,' he says. 'In fact, I'm quite famous in Covent Garden,'

'Yes, true, but you were on your toes for a different reason.'

'Oh, Christ, do you know what. I'd almost forgotten about that,' says Zak as he slumps onto the bed.

'It does seem like a lifetime ago,' I agree. 'Come on, twinkle toes, let's go before Rip comes back.'

'Wonder why he's called Rip. What's it short for?'

'Rip Van Winkle? Maybe he likes his kip,' I giggle.

We've been here for a week now. It's been blissful walking along the beach holding hands like a couple of teenagers. It's even better knowing that Rip is keeping everything shipshape for us.

It would be easy to take advantage of him as he's so eager to please and would work all hours if we let him. But we worked out that in any other circumstances, he would have to pay about £150 per week for a room and food, so we reckoned 10 hours work a week would be fair.

Even though we invite him, he never joins us for meals, preferring to eat in his room.

That suits us. Sometimes he goes out to eat, so we're guessing he has some local friends.

It's so strange to live in an enormous house. I'm finding it a bit spooky, to be honest, but I guess I'll get used to it.

There are so many rooms. It seems a shame to waste them. We even talked about turning it into a B&B or a hotel, but then we remembered that we're on the run and should keep our heads down.

Rip only knows our first names, so we've decided to change our surnames and become Mr and Mrs Channing. No reason for the name. We just saw it on a book cover.

We need to start thinking about money. We don't have much left, and we can't claim benefits. I'm not sure how we could work without revealing our identities.

Despite everything we're not natural criminals.

There are some bits in the house we could sell, but that's a very short-term solution.

So, over dinner one night, we have a brainstorming session.

We have a few business ideas, but they would all involve opening a bank account, and banks are very hot on ID.

It would have to be a cash only business. But that means face to face transactions, and who knows when Mr Plod might decide to take his holidays here?

I suggest maybe we're being overcautious, but Zak reminds me we are not in the first flush of youth, and if we went to prison, we probably wouldn't see the light of day again.

Intellectually, we know this house is ours, or at least Zak's, but it still feels as though it belongs to Aunt Alice and even Rip. And when we think of selling items of furniture or even paintings, it feels wrong. I make a mental note to ask Rip which items would be a loss to him. He has spent most of his life here, so it's only right.

Zak thinks I'm going soft, but I've always been soft. It was just my darling daughter's death that turned me into a raging bull.

Zak's a softie, too, really. But he would never want to admit it. On paper, we're the spawn of the devil, but we're really just ordinary people.

Today is May 22nd, my grandson's first birthday.

During my failed attempts to gain access to him, the social worker, who was about twelve, let it slip that his adoptive parents had named him Gabriel. That seemed unusual to me, so I Googled it, and apparently, it was the fifth most popular name for boys last year. How times change. I wonder if his new parents are religious.

My little angel, Gabriel. I ache to know where he is and how he's doing. Does he look like my little girl? Or, God forbid, like his father?

I'm wracked with guilt that I never go to my daughter's grave, but it's just too painful, and too far away now. But she never leaves my thoughts. I have to be careful not to let my anger overwhelm me again when I think of her and the way she died. I try to make my mind change the subject.

'What's the matter?' It's Zak. I realise tears are streaming down my cheeks.

I put my arms around his neck. 'It's my grandson's birthday.'

He cuddles me. 'Oh dear. You need a distraction. Come and sit down. Rip's come up with an idea that could make us a little bit of money.'

'Legally?' I ask tearfully.

'Of course, legally! How very dare you!'

'Go on, then,' I say, wiping my eyes.

'The ballroom. Rip says Alice used to take dancing lessons in there. Had quite a thriving little business going. Rip was one of her keenest students, and he reckons he could take classes himself. He could either rent the space from us or give us a percentage of his takings.'

'A few little girls doing pirouettes won't bring in much cash.'

'Rip reckons Alice used to make a small fortune. She did four classes a day, charging each student by the term. Anyway, it's worth a try.'

'And will Rip deal with all the admin and contact with the parents?'

'Of course. We don't use the ballroom, so it might as well be making us a few bob. And we'd be paid in cash, so no problems with bank accounts.'

'Sounds ok.'

'Don't get too enthusiastic.'

'Sorry…' I must stop being a misery or Zak might tire of me, and who could blame him?

It seems Rip has quite a network of friends, as soon, the ballroom becomes busy. Many of Alice's pupils return. Rip has hired a pianist and a sweet young girl dancer who helps him.

I sometimes take a peek at the lessons through the window, and it's so funny to see Rip in ballet tights! Better than a tutu, I suppose.

He finally admitted that he had been nicknamed Rip because his tights ripped mid school performance when he was ten. Poor kid.

We take a small regular rent from him. It doesn't amount to much, but it helps with the shopping.

Life is becoming humdrum. There are only so many walks by the sea that you can do, and household chores are mind numbing. It feels like being retired, but we're too young for that.

I miss Cassie and my other friends. I know Zak misses his mates. But what to do? We can't just go home as if nothing has happened. No, we have to bite the bullet and make a life for ourselves here. After all, we would be the envy of many people, living in a mansion with a sea view, and no work to worry about.

Zak's playing games on Rip's computer, so I go for yet another walk along the seafront. There's no denying it's beautiful. I sit on my usual bench and suddenly realise someone is standing beside me.

'Hello, Verity.'

I swear my heart nearly explodes with shock. I turn to see a man of about my age with a dimply smile. It takes me a second to recognise him as an old flame from my youth, Brad.

'I thought it was you,' he grins. 'I saw you from a distance yesterday. Are you on holiday?'

'Erm, yes,' I stutter. 'You?'

162

'On business, actually. You haven't changed, Verity. The last time I saw you we were still in our teens, but I'd still know you anywhere.' He sits beside me.

My mouth doesn't seem to be working.

Brad continues, 'I heard that you got married?'

'Yes,' I manage, 'but he died.'

'Oh, I'm sorry. Any kids?'

'A daughter. She died too.'

'Verity, I'm so sorry. This isn't going well, is it?! Will you join me for a coffee? There's a place just up the hill.'

I'm in turmoil. It actually is good to see Brad. We only split when he went off for a gap year. We were too young. But I don't want anyone to know I'm here, and who knows who he might tell.

We sit down in the busy tea shop, and Brad buys coffee and cakes. He's still handsome and as charming as ever.

As I start to get over the shock, the conversation begins to flow freely. He tells me he married, but it ended in divorce. He has a son and a daughter, both grown up.

He's here for a few days on business.

'What line are you in?' I ask.

'I'm a police officer,' he says. 'You remember, I always wanted to be a cop? I'm now a detective inspector.'

I have spent so long being in terror of the police that I feel genuinely faint. I grab the table as my head reels.

'Verity, are you ok?'

The voice seems to be coming from another universe. I struggle to get up and stagger to the door.

'Verity, what's the matter? Come and sit down.' He leads me to a chair on the pavement.

As I sit down, my phone rings. I recover enough to answer it. It's Zak.

'Where are you?'

'Um, I'll call you back,' I hang up.

I take a deep breath and look at Brad, my first love: now a threat to my freedom, and Zak's.

Brad looks concerned and bewildered.

'It's ok,' I say, 'I've been dieting. Probably need to eat more.'

'Silly girl. There's nothing of you! Let me get you a proper meal.'

'No, n… I need to get back…'

'You with someone?'

'Um, yes, a girlfriend.' Well, I didn't want him to know I'm with Zak.

'I'll walk you back…'

'No, I'll be fine, honestly. It's been great to see you; thanks for the coffee.'

I turn to leave. Brad gently grabs my arm.

'Verity, I'd like to see you again.' His touch sends shivers down my spine. 'I'll be at the bench again tomorrow at the same time,' he says, 'if you'd like to have a proper catch up, and I'll bring some food so you don't pass out on me!'

I give him a watery smile and leave. He watches me until I turn the corner.

Chapter Sixteen

I decide not to mention Brad to Zak. He'd only panic or get jealous. And I'd get the third degree about what I'd said to him.

Zak is picking at the wallpaper in the sitting room.

He turns as I come in. 'Where've you been? Why couldn't you take my call?'

'I know we live in a Georgian house, but you're beginning to sound like a Georgian husband. I was having a coffee in the Tea Room, and it was too noisy to hear myself speak. What are you doing?'

'This place really needs decorating. The paper's coming off this wall. God knows how long it's been up.'

I suddenly get enthusiastic. I love wallpapering. I decorated my house from top to bottom. It's so rewarding to see a room transformed, and it would be a project.

'Ok,' I say, 'If you or Rip do the painting, I'll do the papering.'

'Really?'

'Yes, but can we afford it?'

'Should be able to, just about.'

'The hard job will be getting all this old stuff off. There are probably several layers of paper, and we don't know how solid the plaster is, and there might be lead paint which is dangerous.'

'Ok, I'll have a word with Rip.'

165

I usually take a walk along the seafront at about 11am while Zac has use of Rip's computer during dance lessons. But today I have to think twice. Brad will be waiting for me. Is his business on the island connected to me and Zak? Or is this a genuine coincidence?

To be honest, I'm aching to see him. I've remembered a lot of moments and songs from our courting days. I don't suppose anyone says courting anymore.

We met at school in year 12, or sixth form as we knew it. We both thought we were very grown up. And at 16, I suppose we were in some ways. We went out for two years, and our families got to know each other well. Many thought there'd be wedding bells, including me, but when we left school at 18, we had to go our separate ways. My family couldn't afford a gap year, but Brad and his older brother went off backpacking around the world, and I went to our local college. We didn't seem to have much in common when he came back.

But seeing him again... hearing his voice...

Well, I always go for a walk at this time, so I'm not doing anything wrong. He might not even be there. But, of course, he is.

He stands as I approach. There's that dimply grin again.

'Hi, skinny,' he says.

Just so you know, I'm actually far from skinny.

'Hi, fatso,' I say for no reason, because he's not fat. We sit on the bench, and he hands me a lunch box.

'Eat. I don't want you going all woozy on me again.'

I don't like to say that I've just stuffed a cooked breakfast. I open the box gingerly. There's a feast of mini rolls with delicious fillings, a chocolate bar and a banana.

I look at his kind face and fall in love with him all over again.

Then he says, 'Do you remember this?'

He holds up his phone and music starts to play. It's 'Call Me' by Blondie. It was our song. I'm overwhelmed and blush. Damn! How embarrassing!

He gives me a hug. His smell is familiar and homely. I feel like a child again. I want to be comforted by the man who could ruin my life. It's madness.

'Are you always this ditzy?' he teases. But I see he's welling up.

Everything comes back to me, our hometown, our school, our parents, our fumbling sex. I just want to go back there.

But we're middle aged. I'm with Zak. Brad's a cop. I'm an accessory to two murders and a bank robbery. I'm on the run.

I pull away from him.

'What is it, Verity? There's something very wrong, isn't there?'

'What do you mean?'

'Well, I'm long enough in the tooth to know when someone's in trouble. Is there anything I can help with?' I give an involuntary laugh. He looks wounded.

'Verity, I'm staying at a hotel just down the road. Come and talk to me.'

I would like nothing more in the world than to have Brad's shoulder to cry on. To tell him the whole awful story. And if he was a plumber or a teacher, I would trust him. But cops are notorious for shopping their own mothers, aren't they? The job comes first.

He can see I'm torn. I'm suddenly feeling so vulnerable. Does he already know my secrets?

'I must go,' I say.

He looks down. 'Okay, but I'll be at the bench tomorrow, same time. Now eat your bloody banana.'

This makes me laugh, and his face crinkles into a grin.

I spend the afternoon with Zac and Rip at a DIY store buying everything we need to decorate the sitting room. Zac is not really interested in the wallpaper, but Rip is in his element, and so am I.

We need to choose something in keeping with the age of the house, so eventually go for a light blue Damask pattern. There's so much to carry, we get a taxi back, but Rip is buying an old car tomorrow, so that will be useful.

I go off into a little daydream about Brad. What was his wife like? Why did they divorce? What are his kids doing?

I notice Zak's in a world of his own, too.

There are no dance classes this morning, so Rip helps me to scrape the old paper off the walls. I'm irritated that Zak doesn't pitch in, but he says he told me that he wasn't into DIY, and he did, but it wouldn't kill him. He's back on the computer.

It's 10.15am, and I'm thinking about my 11am walk. And Brad.

I scrape even harder, and a chunk of plaster comes away from the wall.

'Oh no!' I yell.

'It's okay,' says Rip. 'It's bound to happen in such an old house. I can do plastering.'

'Really?'

'Yes, my friend's a builder. He taught me.'

'Handy friend.'

'Yes.'

As the next sheet of old green paper comes away, I notice some words written on the wall. Rip pulls the next piece away so we can see all of it.

At first glance, it looks like a poem, but maybe not as we know it.

A church bell was Maud
But a chuckaboo
Liked a collie shingles
And times she'd cop a mouse
And when at dizzy age
She was still doing the bear
She loved a door knocker
But not a fly rink
She was shilamalink
But to me umble-cum-stumble
Her secret balsam lies in this corinth
Finders to keep.

Zak appears behind us.

169

'What's that all about?'

'I've no idea,' I say. 'Looks like some sort of old English.'

Rip just shrugs.

I grab a pen and an old envelope and write it down.

'Why don't you Google it, Zak?'

'Why would it be on Google?' he scoffs.

'The words, just Google the words…'

'I could do I suppose…finders to keep sounds interesting.'

I glance at the clock. It's 10.50am.

'I need a break. Time for my constitutional,' I say casually, handing the scribbled 'poem' to Zak.

'I'll carry on then, shall I?' asks Rip.

'Sorry to abandon you, do you mind? I won't be long.'

'No problem, you be as long as you like,' he smiles. Rip is a treasure.

Zak goes back to the computer.

I quickly change out of my decorating jeans and T-shirt into a floaty blue top and white trousers. It's a warm day, and I feel like a teenager on a first date.

When I get to the bench, it's empty. I look at my watch. 11.05am. Surely, he would wait five minutes?

I sit and look along the seafront. No sign of him. People stroll by with their partners or their dogs, one or two of them glance at me and smile.

I go from feeling ecstatic to desolate and remember how I felt when he went off for his gap year. Lost.

But I'm not lost. I have Zak. I'm being stupid.

I start walking slowly back to the house, sometimes glancing back to see if Brad has appeared. Maybe he's been taken ill. He has no way of contacting me. Then I turn back and walk back along the seafront. Brad said he was staying at a hotel nearby. There is only one at this end of the bay.

It doesn't take me long to get there. It's not a grand hotel. Quite ordinary and a bit run down.

There's an elderly man at reception.

'Can I help you, love?'

'I'm looking for Mr Brad Benson...'

'Is he staying here?'

'You tell me. I think he was here.'

'Doesn't ring any bells. I'll look in the book. Could he have been part of the police party?'

'Yes, yes he's a police inspector.'

'Oh, okay, they all left yesterday. Some big panic on in the Met.'

'Do you have a number for any of them?'

'Can't give out numbers, love. You could try ringing the Met.'

'Okay, thanks.'

I make for the door.

'Hang on a minute, lovey, are you Verity Brown?'

I rush back to the desk. 'Yes, yes that's me.'

'There's a letter for you.'

I can't believe it. I take the letter back to the bench to read it.

Dear Verity,

I don't suppose you'll ever get this, but just in case you should think to come to the hotel:

171

I'm so sorry to let you down. I've been called back to London and had no way of contacting you.

I can't get you out of my mind. I hope you'll call me, and we can find a way to get together again.

You were my first love, and I'm hoping you'll be my last.

Brad x

His phone number and email address are underneath.

I take my burner phone from my bag and start to dial, but then stop. I can't let him have this number. How do you make it come up as a private caller? Even then, he would surely know how to trace it and get the number.

I need to think about this. I'm thrilled that he's stated his love for me, but I mustn't get carried away. What about Zak? Zak's in my real world, not this silly fantasy from my youth.

I put the phone and the letter back in my bag and make for home.

Zak is sitting at the kitchen table with pen and paper. He looks quite excited.

'I think I've got it,' he beams. I pull up a chair beside him.

'Listen, "*A church bell was Maud*"... a church bell was a talkative woman,

'"*But a chuckaboo*"...that's a close friend. "*Liked a collie shangles*", that means quarrelling, "*and times she'd cop a mouse*", that means a black eye!

172

'"*When at a dizzy age*", old in other words, "*she was still doing the bea*r", that means courting, "*she loved a door knocker*", that's a beard and moustache, "*but not a fly rink*", that's a bald head!

'"*She was shilamanink*"... that means secret, shady or doubtful. "*But to me, rumble-cum-stumble*"... understood.

'This is the interesting part, "*Her secret balsam is in this Corinth*"... a corinth is a brothel! This house was a brothel! And balsam means money or riches!'

I'm intrigued. 'Maud was a working girl who was a chatterbox and liked a good quarrel, which sometimes landed her with a black eye!'

'Yes, and she was still at it into her old age with men with beards. She was a bit dodgy, but she left her money or valuables in this house!'

'Are you sure you got all this right?' I ask.

'According to various experts on 18th century English online.'

'What does Rip say?'

'I haven't told him yet. He's taking a lesson. I've just come off his computer.'

'We need to get our own computer.'

'I know, it's a pain. But we can't afford one just yet.'

I wander into the sitting room to see how far Rip has got with the wallpaper stripping. He's done two walls, but there's no more writing. We need a clue as to where to look.

And even if there was paper money, it could have been eaten by mice, or not worth anything anymore. But if it was coins or jewellery, that might be a different matter. Could Maud be our saviour?

173

I'm finding it hard to think of anything but Brad, and Zak and I seem to be almost ships that pass in the night. Rip has given him a laptop on permanent loan, so now Zak is glued to it 24/7. And is it my imagination, or is he becoming secretive about what he's doing? When I come into the room, he always closes it down and says he was just finished anyway.

We're having a rare drink together when Rip comes into the sitting room.

'Just wondering when you want to continue with the decorating?' he says. He always looks awkward, like an intruding butler.

Zak gives him his translation of 'the poem' and invites him to join us. Rip is intrigued.

'Rip, you know this house better than anyone. Can you think of any hidey holes?' I ask.

'I had heard rumours that it used to be a brothel,' he says, 'How interesting. There are so many nooks and crannies, I don't know where to start, but I'll give it some thought.'

'Thanks. Let's get on with the decorating tomorrow if you have time?' I said.

'I have quite a few lessons booked in, but my assistant is quite capable of taking them by herself now,' he says.

'Well, if you're sure.'

When Rip's gone, I turn to Zak.

'What if Rip finds the treasure and keeps it to himself?'

'That's an evil thought. Not like you.'

'He knows the house better than we do and has more chance of finding it.'

'It doesn't mean he'd keep it.'

'Would you share it with him if you found it?'

'Nope.'

'Well then.'

'Look, Verity,' he says irritably, 'we don't even know if it exists, or even what it is, so let's cross that bridge if and when we come to it.'

There's an awkward silence. We never have awkward silences. I feel as if I've been told off, shut down.

Zak takes his drink and goes back to his laptop.

I stare at the half-prepared walls and am not looking forward to more wallpaper scraping tomorrow.

I've decided I can't risk phoning Brad from my burner phone and wonder if phone boxes still exist. I haven't been inside one for years. Do they work on change or credit cards? I'll try to find one tomorrow.

We get cracking bright and early in the morning, Rip and I both scraping old wallpaper.

We chat about where the 'treasure' might be located, although, truth be told, neither of us really believe it. But it's fun to speculate.

Just before 11am, Rip goes to check on his classes, and I can't wait a minute longer to ring Brad. With my usual excuse of taking my constitutional, I grab my bag and leave.

I decide to walk along the seafront to the village. I've never noticed a phone box, but then I've never looked for one before.

As I round the corner, I get the shock of my life. Brad is sitting on our bench.

I stop dead, and he grins at me. He pats the seat beside him.

I feel myself blushing. What an idiot. A middle-aged teenager! I sit down with a big grin on my face, wondering what my hair looks like and trying to remember if I cleaned my teeth this morning.

Brad takes my hand and says quietly, 'You didn't ring me.'

'No, I was going to…'

'But?'

'It's complicated.'

'Yes, I know.'

I look at him, what does he know?

'Verity, I know all about it.'

'All about what?'

'When I got back to London, I did a bit of digging. Only because I couldn't stop thinking about you. I put your name into the computer, and guess what came up?'

I start to feel woozy again.

'Oh no you don't go fainting on me again… here,' he reaches in his pocket, 'Have a banana.'

'I'm not a bloody chimp.'

'No, you're a bloody chump! Verity, you have nothing to fear from me. I'm due to retire soon and have been disillusioned with the job for years now. I love you. I've always loved you, and if you're in trouble, I'm here to help.'

'How?'

'Well, let's have some lunch and talk about it.'

Is this a trap? I know who the old Brad was, but is this new Brad on the level? Can I take the risk?

But then again, if he already knows everything…

We find a quiet restaurant and sit in a corner. We both order a crab salad with crusty bread and a pot of tea.

I look across the table at the man I fell in love with when I was sixteen. His hair is now greying, and his brown eyes now have laughter lines, but his face is still handsome and his smile irresistible.

I feel dowdy in my jeans and T-shirt, but he doesn't seem to notice.

'So, young lady, tell me all about it.'

'Oh no, you tell me what you know.'

'Well, according to the police computer, you are wanted for questioning about being an accomplice in a murder and a bank robbery.'

I look down and blush. Damn. It sounds so awful. I don't know what to say.

'Verity, nobody knows I'm seeing you. I'm not going to arrest you. I know you; there must be a story to this.'

'He killed my daughter and half killed her baby,' I say quietly.

He nods. 'Did you play a part in killing him?'

'No, he came to my house looking for trouble and my friend had to restrain him….it got out of hand…'

'But then he was buried in a wood. Why not just report it as self-defence? The man was known to be violent.'

'I told you, it's complicated.'

'Because of the bank robbery? Where do you come into that?'

'It's a long story.'

In for a penny, in for a pound. I'm aware that he could be taping me, but I tell him everything. It's a huge relief to get it all off my chest.

He sits back and looks at me. I can't tell what he's thinking.

He orders another pot of tea.

Eventually, he says, 'So you're still living with this guy?'

'Yes.'

'Do you love him?'

Since we're being honest, I say, 'Not as much as I love you,' but I immediately feel disloyal and stupid. He looks at me again, deep in thought.

'I need to think this through,' he says. 'Can we meet again tomorrow?'

Now that I've told him everything, I feel more at ease but at the same time full of shame and embarrassment. How can he ever see me as the old decent Verity again? And is he weighing up whether to put the job first or me? Especially now he knows I'm living with Zak.

'Yes, we could meet here again if you like.'

'Can I have your phone number?'

I hesitate. 'Ok, it's a burner. I'll only use it to text you if necessary. I don't want to lose touch with you again.'

'Okay.'

We agree to meet the next day and go our separate ways.

I'm worried and elated at the same time as I make my way home.

Rip has finished the scraping and is preparing the paintwork. He says Zak has gone to get a paper.

I wander into the kitchen to put the kettle on and see the laptop open on the table. I tap it into life and up comes a dating site.

So, that's what Zak's been doing. He's been talking to a woman called Miranda, and he's told her he's single!

I leave it as I found it and go straight out again.

I make my way back to the bench and look out to sea. The waves are gently lapping onto the smooth sand, and I always find it soothing.

I wander onto the beach, and to the water's edge. I take off my sandals and let the cool water lap over my feet.

My mind is a jumble of Zak, Brad, decorating, and the mysterious hidden belongings of a prostitute called Maud.

I think of the picture of Miranda on the dating site. She's not glamorous, but young and pretty in a natural way.

It's probably my fault. I've been so obsessed with Brad. I've been taking Zak for granted. Has he really gone out to get a paper, or is he meeting Miranda?

I'm hurt, but I can't get on my high horse because I've been seeing Brad. But I didn't go looking for Brad.

It suddenly hits me like a thunderbolt that there is now a policeman who knows everything and where we are. I have really let my guard down. I feel panicky. Zac would go mad if he knew.

I have spent my life trusting people. Now I don't know who to trust. Zac must be really unhappy with me to go onto dating sites.

I stroll back to the house. Rip is making a great job of the painting. There's a lot of coving and skirting, not to mention the doors to be painted, but he's getting there.

Zac is still out. I think he should be helping Rip, but I'm more concerned about where he is.

I get a coffee for Rip and a cold drink for myself and sit and watch him work. I don't feel guilty because I'll be doing all the papering.

Rip starts painting a section of skirting board when a piece comes loose. He looks at me apologetically.

'It's ok, Rip. It's an old house. That can be fixed back again.'

'But there's a hole behind it,' he says.

'It can be filled.'

'Yes, I can fill it, but there's something in there.'

'Like what?' I ask.

Rip pushes his hand into the hole. I put down my drink and kneel beside him. He pulls out a dirty leather pouch about the size of an orange and looks at me.

'Oh my God, Rip, open it!'

Rip carefully pulls it open and turns it upside down on the carpet. A handful of colourless stones fall out.

We look at each other. I pick up one of the stones.

'Surely they couldn't be diamonds?' I ask.

'Could be glass or paste,' says Rip.

'Maud's treasure.'

'Could be,' says Rip shyly. 'Since we saw the writing, I've been looking into the history of the area. The girls used to get paid by the sailors who came from India and South Africa, and pirates used to come to beaches near here. They could have been paid in gemstones.'

'What's all this?' It's Zac, minus newspaper.

I grab a few stones and rush to show him, singing, 'Diamonds are a girl's best friend!'

'Are they diamonds?' he asks.

'Don't know but could be. Rip just found them hidden in the skirting.'

'Blimey, so Maud did have some goodies.'

'Looks like it.'

We pick them all up and take them to the kitchen table for a closer look.

They vary in size from a pea to a small pebble. There are 34 of them.

Zac gets a glass of water. It must be the shock, but no, he picks up the stones and drops them all into the glass.

'What are you doing?' I ask.

'If they're fake, they'll float,' he says, 'but if they sink, they're diamonds.'

They all sink.

'Are you sure? How do you know that?'

'I don't know, I read it somewhere.'

Rip says, 'I'll get back to the painting,' and leaves.

'Shouldn't you be helping him?' I ask. 'The deal was that you two do the painting, and I'd do the papering.'

'Yeah, yeah, in a minute. What shall we do with these?' He's peering into the glass. 'She must have been a busy girl, this Maud.'

'Yes, she must have been,' I say. 'And have you been a busy boy?'

'What do you mean?'

I click on the open laptop, and the dating page is still there.

Zac looks sheepish. 'I was just mucking about, got a bit bored,' he says.

'Bored with me, obviously.'

'Don't be stupid.'

'I'm stupid for thinking that you being on a dating site means you'd rather be with someone else?!'

'I'm not having this conversation,' says Zak, as he leaves the room.

Bloody typical! He insults me for being upset at his behaviour. Why can men never apologise and accept when they are in the wrong?

I hear the front door slam. So now he's probably going to see HER.

It's now 9am, and Zac has been out all night.

And the diamonds have disappeared. After he went out, I put them back in their pouch and hid them in a biscuit tin where I keep the cash that Rip gives us. Zac is the only one who knows about the tin. He must have been back while I was asleep.

Does that mean he's left me?

I rush to look in his wardrobe. A few bits and pieces are missing along with his shaving kit and soap bag.

He's bloody well moving in with her!

I'm overwhelmed with hurt and anger. Zac and I have been through a lot together and even knew each other for years before getting together. He's Cassie's brother, for God's sake. He's my best friend. Was my best friend.

I try to ring him, but his phone is switched off.

As I wander back into the kitchen, Rip appears.

'Mrs Channing, can I speak to you, please?'

'Of course, Rip, what is it?'

'Well, last night, in the early hours I heard a noise, and when I got to the top of the stairs, I could see Mr Channing in the hall with my laptop. It's ok, I said he could borrow it, but he left the house with it, so I was a bit concerned, and I followed him.'

'Yes? Where did he go?'

'He went to the Bay Hotel. I waited, but he didn't come out again.'

'It's okay, Rip, we had a bit of a row last night. I'm sure he'll be back when he calms down. Do you need the laptop urgently?'

'Oh no, but I will need it back. It has some work stuff on it.'

'Don't worry, I'll see you get it back.'

Great. So, Zac is in the same hotel as Brad and is probably with his floozie.

Brad! I must get ready to see Brad.

I take a shower, try to make my hair look presentable and put on a flowery linen dress and strappy sandals.

Brad is on our bench looking tanned and smelling gorgeous. The sea air must be doing him good.

He looks out to sea as I sit down.

'I really could get used to this,' he says. Then he turns to me. 'What's the matter?'

'The matter?'

'Yes, I can always tell. Has something happened?'

'I found Zac on a dating site, we had a row, and he spent the night in your hotel, probably with a woman.'

'Oh,' he sighs. 'I'm sorry to hear that. What now?'

'You tell me.'

'Ok, I've been giving this a lot of thought,' he says. 'I'm due to retire in two months. I'm not at retiring age, of course, but we retire after 25 years in the job. I'll still need to work. If we decided to get together, we could do so after I retire, but I would have to deny all knowledge of your... shall we say... misdemeanours if I was ever challenged.'

'Of course.'

'As far as Zac's concerned, I'd be surprised if the police didn't catch up with him at some stage, but he might be lucky. But there's always the risk that if he goes down, so do you.

'Verity, if I didn't know you the way I do, I wouldn't dream of taking this view, but to me you're a grieving mother and the victim of circumstances.

184

'It's up to you now to decide what you want to do. You have a lovely home here with Zak. I couldn't offer you anything as grand. But we could buy a little place somewhere and make a new life.

'But I'd need to know that you and Zak are over for good.'

It all sounds like a bit of a business arrangement, but I suppose Brad is used to speaking in a formal way with his work. It seems like a rehearsed speech, but as he says, he's been giving it a lot of thought.

Am I still in love with the teenage Brad? Do I really know this man?

'You've gone quiet,' he says, looking concerned.

'Sorry, just thinking…'

He takes my hands in his and looks into my eyes just as Zak comes round the corner.

Chapter Seventeen

Zak has his arm around the girl from the dating site, and they are laughing and joking together. I realise I haven't seen Zak laugh in a while.

When he sees me, he stops dead. He says something to the girl, and she glances at me and then heads back towards the hotel.

Brad catches on quickly and stands up. I stay seated on the bench and say nothing.

Zak looks from me to Brad and then turns and heads back the way he came.

I suddenly realise I'm shaking.

'Come on,' says Brad. 'It looks like he's made the decision for you. Why don't we go back to your place, pick up your stuff and go back to London? You could stay with my daughter until I retire, and then we can get a place together wherever you like.'

This is all happening so quickly, my head's spinning. But maybe he's right. I don't know if and when Zak will return, and if he does, it's his house, not mine. I realise that the diamonds are his too. They were in his house.

But why would I want to stay with Brad's daughter? I've never even met her, and she might not want a stranger foisted on her.

We stroll back to the house, both in our own thoughts.

Rip is in the sitting room with a paintbrush in his hand. He puts it down as we enter.

'Rip, this my friend Brad; Brad, this is Rip, amazing painter and dancer!'

'Hello, sir.'

'Just Brad is fine. Looks like you're doing a great job.'

'Thanks, I've just about finished.'

'Rip, I'm going away for a little while. I expect Zak will be back soon, but as you know, he's at the Bay Hotel if you need him.'

'Don't worry, I'll look after the place. How long will you be away?'

I look at Brad. 'I'm not sure yet. But I'll let you know.'

I pack a bag and we're at the front door when Zak runs up the drive. He's staggering slightly. He sees my bag.

'Don't leave me, Verity, please. I know I've been stupid, a real idiot, but I love you, we love each other. We've been through so much...Verity, please don't go.'

He's a strong man, ex-army, but now he looks like a crumpled little boy.

I don't know what to do or say, so I say nothing. Brad just waits for my response.

Zak looks at Brad. 'Who is this guy? Are you leaving me for him? Someone you've just met?'

I look at Brad.

'It's your decision,' he says softly.

I see the anger rising in Zak. 'Didn't take you long, did it?'

'You had gone off with some woman to a hotel, so don't come the high and mighty with me!' I spit.

'And I'd only been gone five minutes when you find someone to shack up with.'

Brad steps in, 'Let's calm down, shall we. I think maybe we've had a few too many…'

'You keep out of it, pal. She's not coming with you.'

'She'll make her own mind up,' Brad says evenly.

'I told you to shut the fuck up!' Zak takes a swing at Brad. Brad bars him and twists his arm up his back, but Zak kicks out and catches Brad awkwardly, causing him to lose his balance and fall heavily, hitting his head on the doorstep, where he lays still.

I rush to see if he's okay, and Zak looks on.

I look up and see Rip standing in the doorway, shaking. 'Shall I call an ambulance, Mrs Channing?'

'No,' says Zak. 'No, it's ok, Rip, he'll be fine. You go back to what you were doing.'

Rip looks to me for confirmation. There's blood coming from a wound on Brad's head.

'Maybe you could get some water and a towel?'

'Of course,' says Rip, and he scurries off.

'You idiot!' I yell at Zak. 'Why did you do that?'

Zak is slurring his words now. 'Don't leave me. You were going to leave me…'

'Get him inside,' I snap.

Zak lifts Brad in an unsteady fireman's lift and staggers into the sitting room. He lays him on the sofa.

'I just hope you haven't killed him,' I cry.

'Wouldn't want your precious boyfriend to pop off, would we?'

'What is the matter with you, Zak? God, you've changed!'

Rip comes in with a bowl of water and a towel.

'Thanks, Rip, could you get a strong coffee for Zak, please?'

Rip looks at Zak and at Brad and rushes off again.

Zak slumps into a chair.

'Zak, what are we going to do? This man needs to be in hospital!'

'Are you going to go off with him?'

'Do you not care that you've half-killed a man?'

I start to clean up the wound. There is no response from Brad.

'I've killed lots of men,' says Zak, just as Rip comes into the room. He looks horrified, puts down the coffee and leaves.

'Who is he, anyway?' asks Zak.

'Does it matter? Drink your coffee.'

I can usually count on Zak to help me, but he's drunk and jealous and useless. I have to deal with this on my own, but how? Poor lovely Brad...

I so want to call an ambulance, but it would land us both in jail. I decide we should put him somewhere outside and then call an ambulance.

He could have been attacked in the street. Then I feel his pulse. Nothing.

I let him die rather than go to jail. I'll never forgive myself. Whatever happened to the Verity I used to be?

I look at the lifeless body of the man I used to love and sob until I'm empty.

Zak is in a drunken sleep.

It's Chester all over again. Except I was glad to see the back of him, God forgive me.

Rip wanders in.

'Mrs Channing, he's... dead, isn't he?'

I nod.

Great, not only do I have a dead cop in my sitting room, but I have a witness too.

'What am I going to do, Rip?'

'You should call the police. That's the right thing to do.'

'But Zak would be in big trouble.'

'Hitting his head on the step was an accident. I don't think Mr Channing meant for him to die,' says Rip.

'I'm sure you're right, but Mr Channing has had too much to drink, and we can't get the police just yet. Don't worry, Rip, I'll call them soon.'

He nods and leaves the room.

You're probably thinking that Zak is a monster, and I should shop him, but he's not a monster. Stupid at times, yes, and his army training kicks in, but he had good reason to hit back at Chester, and today he's drunk and jealous and just wanted to give his rival a smack. No excuse, I know, and he shouldn't have done it, but he's not a murderer. And despite everything, I still love him.

I give Brad a tearful hug and say my goodbyes, and then cover him with a blanket. There's no point in trying to get any sense out of Zak for a few hours yet.

The shock of it all is just setting in, so I have a large brandy to settle my nerves. And then another.

I wake up to see the sun streaming through the windows. I'm still in an armchair in the sitting room. There is no sign of Zak...or Brad.

My head is throbbing, so I make for the kitchen to get some water and pain killers.

I hear the piano playing in the ballroom. Rip must be taking a lesson.

I go back into the sitting room and try to clear my head. Where's Zak? And more importantly, where's Brad?

I wander out into the garden, and then out to the front of the house. I then go back in and check upstairs. No sign of anyone.

I make some coffee and sit back down. I try to phone Zak, but there's no reply. Then I have an idea. I'll ring Brad's number. Zak must have gone through his pockets... then SHIT! It hits me. Zak will have discovered that Brad is, was a policeman. Did he think I was setting him up? Does he think I was set up? Now I'm even more worried.

The piano stops, and after a few minutes, Rip appears at the door.

'Are you alright, Mrs Channing? I was worried about you. I couldn't wake you up.'

'I'm fine, thanks, Rip, just a bit hungover. Where's Mr Channing?'

'I took him and the, er, gentleman to the undertakers. He said he would walk back.'

'Really, the undertakers? What time was that?'

'This morning, I tried to wake you. It was before my class, about 9 o'clock.'

I glance at the clock. It's 11.05am.

Rip gives me a caring smile and leaves.

192

Where can Zak be? I can't believe he would take the body to an undertaker. Too many questions would be asked.

Maybe he's gone off with his new girlfriend. He said he wanted to be with me, but that was before he knew Brad was a cop.

I feel a bit panicky. Maybe I should leave. I already have my bags packed from yesterday.

But where would I go? I don't have a lot of money.

I notice Zak has left his jacket on the back of the sofa. I feel in his pockets. He must have taken his wallet with him, there's nothing, except...the diamonds!

That'll do. I wouldn't be in this situation if he wasn't so handy with his fists. I feel defensive because I'm afraid he'll be angry about Brad, but I'm also hurt and angry about his 'girlfriend'.

I put the diamonds in my bag just as Zak walks in the room.

He stands at the doorway and looks at me.

'Did you know that guy was a police inspector from the Met?'

'Yes, I did. But he was ok. He was my first boyfriend when I was a teenager,' I feel the tears threatening.

'So, how come you were with him?'

'We just bumped into each other on the seafront. I hadn't seen him in all those years.'

Zak knows I'm telling the truth. I'm not a liar unless I have to be.

'Well, it's sorted anyway.'

'What have you done?'

193

Zak brightens, 'I had a brainwave. I swapped identities with him. I took him to the undertakers, and said I was a police officer, showed his ID, and said that the body was me. I put my ID in his pocket.'

'What ID, not your passport?'

'No, just a couple of out-of-date credit cards, AA membership etc. Worked like a charm. They weren't going to question a senior cop, were they?' Zac looks pleased with himself. 'And the bonus is, I am now officially dead!'

'But surely the police don't just carry bodies into the undertakers without a coffin or something?'

'I said he'd been in an accident, hence the head wound.'

'But wouldn't he have been taken to hospital, put in the morgue. There'd be an inquest and ….'

'I just cut out the middleman,' laughed Zak. 'You worry too much. You always have.'

'I don't think we should hang about here, do you?'

'Probably not. Do you want a coffee?'

'I'm ok, thanks.'

While Zak is making himself a coffee, I slip the diamonds back into his pocket and feel guilty for taking them. Surprising how panic can take over.

When he comes back, I ask him why he was out for so long.

'Oh,' he says, sipping his coffee, 'I went to the Bay Hotel. I had the cop's hotel key, so I went to his room. Very useful. I got his passport and his laptop. Oh, and his driving licence. There were some car keys from a rental company, but I couldn't find the car, and anyway, it's too traceable, so I chucked them. I've also got the keys that were in his pocket, but they're probably for his house and maybe work. Do you know his address?'

'NO!'

'Ok, okay.'

'What have we become? You're acting like a hardened criminal.'

'We have no choice! We *are* criminals. We have to be hard to survive. It's that or just give ourselves up. Then we could be our real lovely selves in prison for the rest of our lives.'

The sad thing is, I know he's right.

Two hours later, we're on the ferry to the mainland. Then we go to Southampton airport and get a flight to Antwerp. Where else would you go with a pocket full of diamonds?

It's only a short flight, but I can't help thinking about poor Brad. And his daughter and son. Amid the sadness, I feel anger towards Zac, and resentment.

I will always treasure the letter that Brad left for me at the hotel, but I have to try to put it all behind me now.

After trudging around for a while, we find a reasonably priced hotel.

It's my first time in Antwerp, and I'm in tourist mode.

We unpack the essentials and go for a wander. I'm stunned by the beautiful buildings. I don't know what I'd expected. I've never given Antwerp a thought.

We find a pavement cafe overlooking the river. It's busy, but we manage to get a table with a canopy next to the water's edge. The sun's shining, and we smile at each other. The stress of the last few days has lifted a little, and it's time to relax. We'll seek out a diamond merchant tomorrow, but we know that the diamonds are money in the bank, so we don't need to worry about money for a while.

A woman at the next table keeps looking at me. After a while she grins. I mutter to Zak while pretending to look at my phone but tell him not to look around.

Then the woman gets up and comes to our table.

'You don't recognise me, do ya?'

'I'm sorry, I…'

'Well, why should ya?' she laughs. 'I'm just the cleaner. You was the lady who came into the social worker's office and gave them some stick! Good on ya.'

'I think you must be confusing me with someone else,' I say, feeling my stomach lurch.

'Nah, it was you, don't you remember? You was upset coz they wouldn't let you have your grandbaby. They had a bloody cheek if you ask me, giving him to that Trish woman instead of his own granny.'

'You work in the Hertsway Social Services office?'

'Yes, that's what I'm saying, I'm the cleaner. I remember you, coz you was hoppin' mad. Small world, ain it?'

'It certainly is; what are you doing here?'

'Me and me other arf have got a camper van, and we're doing Europe. He's just getting coffees. Did you 'ave any luck with seeing your kid?'

196

'No, I didn't.'

'Bloody shame. Here's Eric. Eric, this is the lady I told you about. They took her grandson and give 'im to someone else.'

Eric puts down the coffees and reaches out his hand.

'Alright?'

We both say, 'Hello, Eric,' and shake hands.

'Eric, give 'em your card. You never know when they might need a plumber, and put my number on it an 'all in case they need a cleaner.'

Eric does as he's told and hands me the card.

'Why don't we meet up for tea tonight?' she says.

Zac jumps straight in. 'Er that would be lovely, but we're off later today.'

'Ah, never mind. Take care. I 'spect I'll see ya around.'

'Yes, good to see you,' I add, smiling.

They go back to their table, and we leave, giving them a wave.

We stride back towards the hotel.

'For God's sake, is nowhere safe?' snarls Zac.

'She knows who's got Gabriel,' I say quietly.

'Don't start going down that route again!'

I stop walking and look at Zak, 'He's my bloody grandson, my daughter's baby. My flesh and blood. If I can find a way to see him, I will!'

'Okay, calm down. I just don't want to see you upsetting yourself again.'

We walk on in silence, Zak worried about us being discovered and me thinking about Gabriel and wondering who 'Trish' is.

Somehow, Antwerp is not somewhere you'd expect to bump into people you know. Spain maybe, Paris perhaps, but Antwerp…

As we make our way through a built-up area to our hotel, Zak suddenly stops.

'That's the place, the diamond place. I looked it up, it's the GIA, Gemmological Institute of America or something. They have labs where they make diamonds. It's amazing, isn't it.'

'I didn't know you could manufacture diamonds,' I say.

'No, but they do, apparently. Let's go in and see what they say about ours.'

'Won't we need an appointment?'

'Don't know, but it's worth a try.'

Zac goes to the door where two men are standing, chatting.

He turns back to me, 'They speak Dutch here, don't they?' One of the men overhears.

'Yes, we speak Dutch, but also English. Can I help you?'

'Um, yes, please. We would like to speak with someone from the GIA.'

'I am a manager here. What can I help you with?'

Zac is cautious. 'Can we go in, off the street?'

'Ok.' The man excuses himself from his friend and takes us inside.

We are taken into a small office.

Zac reaches into his pocket and brings out the pouch with the stones. He tips them onto the desk and looks at the man.

The man takes a jeweller's magnifying glass from his desk drawer and picks up the stones one by one to inspect them.

Finally, he says, 'What do you want to do with them?'

'We want to sell them,' says Zac.

'As they are?'

'Well, yes.'

'And you want to know what they're worth?'

'Yes, please.'

'Ok, well, it's all to do with the colour and marks and inclusions. If it's a colourless stone it goes into category D...it starts at D, there is no A, B or C. If you have something that's 2grams and 5carat that could be worth ...in sterling...up to £100,000.'

We gasp and look at each other.

'But without closely examining all of these, it's hard to say. I doubt any of them are in that league. If you're just looking for a quick sale, the most I could offer you would be £30,000.'

'For all of them?' I ask.

'Yes, they could be worth very little.'

'Surely, more than that for 34 diamonds?' says Zak.

'Ok, look I'll go to £40,000, but that would definitely be my final offer. I doubt you'd get that anywhere else, but you're welcome to try. I'd need to see some ID.'

He leaves the room for us to discuss it.

'Let's face it,' says Zak. 'We have no idea what they're worth, and they didn't cost us anything.'

'Yes, a bird in the hand and all that. What about the ID?'

'I'll give the copper's ID.'

That gives me a stab in my heart and an instant picture of Brad lying bleeding on the doorstep.

'Ok. What if they check it out?'

'I can't use my real ID. We'll have to risk it.'

The man returns. 'Do you want to go ahead? I'll need your bank details.'

'I'd prefer cash,' says Zac confidently.

The man looks hard at him.

'Can I see your ID, please?'

Zac brings out Brad's driving licence and police warrant card. The images are small, and Zac holds his breath. At a glance, he is not unlike Brad.

The demeanour of the man changes. 'Oh, you're a police officer. No problem, sir.'

He leaves the room.

'Do you think he'll have that much cash on the premises? If not, we might have to wait for another day, and we can't take the risk of him checking…' I'm panicking.

'Shhhhh,' says Zak.

The man returns with a bulky envelope.

'It's in Euros, of course. Is that ok?'

'Yes, that's fine. Thanks.'

'Please sign here.'

Zac signs and gets up to leave.

'It's a pleasure doing business with you,' he says. He really does have a lot of bottle.

Chapter Eighteen

Back in the hotel room, we get the giggles and throw the money around like confetti. It may not be life changing, but it will keep us going for a while if we're careful.

Zak lays on the bed surrounded by Euros and looks at me.

'So, honeybun, what's next?' he asks.

'I've no idea. But maybe we should move on from here now that our friend from the social services office has seen us.'

'Yes, bloody woman. We'll probably go to Outer Mongolia and bump into Cassie!'

'Speaking of Cassie, I think we should go back for a little while and see how she's doing. She's been holding the fort for us for ages, and now she needs to take over the house in the Isle of Wight if we're not going back there.'

'You want to take that risk?'

'Just briefly. We could stay with Cassie so we're not seen at my house.'

I have an ulterior motive, of course. I want to track down this Trish woman and my grandson.

When Zak's in the shower, I find the card that the cleaner gave me. It's Eric the plumber's card, but her number is there too. I don't think she mentioned her name, but it's here, Sally.

I dial the number using the hotel phone.

'Hello.'

'Hi, is that Sally?'

'Yes?'

'It's Verity here, we met yesterday…'

'Oh yes, the lady who had a go at the social workers,' she laughs.

'Yes, that's me. I wondered, when will you be going home?'

'We're heading back today, actually. Eric's got a big job on. We were planning to stay for a few more days, but they need 'im. We've been away for three weeks now, so we 'aven't done bad. Why? Did you want a cleaner?'

'I might do,' I lie, 'I thought maybe we could meet up and talk about it?'

'Yeah, no problem. Do you know the Red Lion at Cottbridge? They do a lovely dinner.'

'Yes, I know it.' My heart sinks, it's a dive. 'What about Wednesday?'

'One o'clock?'

'Oh, you mean lunch...yes, yes that's fine.'

We arrive on Cassie's doorstep the next day. She's shocked but pleased to see us. There are hugs and kisses, and she faffs around trying to find something to give us to eat.

It feels great to be home. There may not be much sunshine or beaches, but home is home, and nothing can beat it.

As far as she's concerned, we've just been on an extended holiday. We skirt around her many questions and tell her that the Isle of Wight was great for a holiday, but we don't want to live there. We'll discuss what we can do with the place later.

Cassie is happy for us to stay, but she stresses that she's been looking after my house, so can't understand why we don't want to go there.

It's not easy to find a reason. We make light of it and say we just want to spend time with her as we haven't seen her for ages.

It's Wednesday, and Zak's gone to see his mates. Luckily, Cassie has an art class, so I don't have to explain my absence.

Sally is waiting for me at The Red Lion sitting at the bar happily chatting to the barman.

My feet stick to the floor as we find a table.

'The nosh is great here, ain't it, Dave?' she shouts to the barman.

'What are you 'aving, darlin'?' he shouts back.

'I'll 'ave sausage, egg an' chips. What do you want, Verity?'

I really, really don't want to eat here, but it'll be worth getting salmonella to see my grandson.

'Um, I'll have the same,' I smile.

Surprisingly, the food arrives quickly and is fine.

'Do you want me to clean for ya?' she asks with a mouthful of chips.

'To be honest, Sally, no. But I do want you to do something for me. You mentioned that my grandson is with a woman called Trish…'

Sally looks crestfallen. She must be short of work.

'Sally, I will make it worth your while if you help me find my little Gabriel. It means everything to me. I've lost my only child, and I have no other family. Please.'

Sally looks at me and then stuffs a sausage into her mouth.

'What do you want to know?'

'Where he is, who he's with, anything, everything.'

'I shouldn't 'ave said nuffin. I could lose me job.'

'It would be our secret. I promise. Look, if I do anything to make you lose your job, I'll pay you a year's wages.'

She perks up. 'A year's?'

'Yes, what do you earn, how many hours do you work?'

'I work 15 hours a week, and I get 150 quid.'

'Ok, if you get the sack because of me I'll give you £7,500.'

'Well…'

'And if you tell me his address and the name of his adoptive parents, I'll give you £1000.'

'Oh, he's not adopted yet. He's with foster parents.'

This knocks the wind out of me. 'Not adopted, but I was told…'

'He is up for adoption, but it all takes ages,'

'How do you know this?'

'I hear bits and pieces, but I know Trish. She's been fostering for ages and often comes into the office. No one takes no notice of me doin' me cleanin'.'

'So, you know the address?'

'Nah. But it will be in the file.'

'Surely that will be computerised. How would you get into it?'

Sally laughs as she stuffs the last chip into her mouth. 'They still have filing cabinets and paper files. They do lock 'em when they remember, but the keys are just in the desk drawer. It's pathetic really.'

'You could find out?'

'I could try.'

'Would you?'

I think of my darling daughter, Melody, and to my embarrassment, tears start to fall onto my plate.

Sally looks at me sympathetically. 'I'll do me best. I think they thought you was flaky because you had such a go at them, but I knew you was grieving and desperate.'

'Thanks, Sally,' I sniffle, blowing my nose and forcing a smile. 'This must be our secret, of course.'

'Course. What will you do if you find out where he is?'

'I'm not sure yet. One day at a time, eh?'

I feel wrung out and stuffed when I get back to Cassie's. I felt duty-bound to eat the food and have to admit it was good, but there was too much of it.

The first thing Cassie says is, 'I wondered where you'd got to. You must be hungry. Perfect timing, I've made you some sausage, egg and chips.'

Luckily, Zak, the bottomless pit, arrives and makes short work of the food.

When Cassie goes to bed, Zak says we should move on. It's too dangerous to stay on home ground.

205

I know he's right, but I have to be here now. Maybe I could adopt my grandson after all...if I could convince them... hell, I shouldn't have to convince anyone, he's MY flesh and blood.

But if I put my head above the parapet and they do police checks...

I suppose we could move on, as long as we're not too far away. I could come back when I hear from Sally. But where to go?

Zak says he has an old army buddy called Bunter who lives in Cambridge. He's divorced but still lives in the family home as his wife ran off with a wealthy stockbroker.

'He has plenty of room and would welcome the company,' says Zak.

'Bunter?'

'He's a bit on the porky side. I don't think I ever knew his real name.'

'Can you trust him?'

'With my life.'

'Do they let porky people in the army?'

'Now, now, don't be fattist! He's a top bloke; you'll love him.'

That was two days ago. Now here we are in a Victorian terraced house in Cambridge.

Zak was right. Bunter is a lovely bloke. Huge, but lovely. We have a large spare room overlooking a park. The whole house is beautifully decorated and modern, not in keeping with its Victorian heritage, but extremely comfortable and practical.

But dammit, it's not home. We can't keep moving from pillar to post. It's crazy. But for now, we have no option and at least have the luxury of a comfortable bed and some money.

We do the tourist bit for a few days, even taking a punt on the river. There are some interesting little shops and restaurants, and people watching is fun from pavement cafes.

There are some cruel traffic calming measures which are amusing to watch. If you accidentally drive down a bus lane, for instance, a pole comes out of the road and lifts your car into the air! Maybe good revenge but does nothing to speed the flow of traffic!

This has all been something of a distraction, so I'm surprised when my burner phone rings. It's Sally.

Luckily, Zak has gone walkabout. He likes to look at all the old buildings.

'Sally.'

'Yes, can't talk long. I'm in the office.'

'Okay.'

'The foster mum lives at 4 Station Terrace. She's a single mum with a kid of her own. Have to go,' she hangs up.

I'm in shock. I have the address. I know where my baby is. I must work out how to see him. Not for the first time, I wonder if he looks like my daughter and hope he doesn't take after his father.

I can't tell Zak about this. He'd find a way of stopping me. I'll go tomorrow.

We haven't dared use our cars, so we have no transport. It will have to be the train. But as I'm going to Station Terrace, there won't be too far to walk.

I'm excited and somehow terrified. Terrified of myself. Terrified of what I might do. The overwhelming love for a child and the need to protect my daughter's baby is unbearable.

I wish they hadn't called him Gabriel. My grandson would not have been called Gabriel. He would have been Sam or Tom.

So, the social workers thought I was flaky because I was distraught! What do they know? Most of them look about twelve and have had no life experience. And why do they let a child stay with a foster parent only to rip him away from the only mother he's known to give him to someone else? Maybe not so bad if they're still babes in arms, but it can take years. My poor lamb.

I'll have to think of something to tell Zak. He'll want to know where I'm going.

I've told Zak I'm going to catch up with a few old friends. He tells me to be careful and seems quite happy to have a day to himself. He and Bunter will probably do some blokey things. Bunter seems happy to have Zak to himself for the day.

My heart is pounding as I catch an early train to my hometown. Station Terrace is the other side of town and a good few miles from my house, so I don't know the area well.

The train is busy, and I have to stand. This is a momentous day for me. I look at the other passengers and wonder if this journey is special for any of them? Maybe meeting their birth mother for the first time or on their way to an important job interview. But maybe it's just another groundhog day as they make their way to the office.

As I get off the train, my thoughts are just with Gabriel. He'll be toddling now. I wonder how old Trish's child is.

Luckily, 4 Station Terrace is only a few metres from the station. It's one of a small terrace of cottages, probably built for railway workers way back when. There is no front garden, and the windows have nets. I walk to the end of the row to see if I can look into the back gardens, but it's impossible. There are high fences and hedges and they back onto the railway lines. Not a great place to live.

Now what do I do? I could knock with some pretence, or I could sit in the pub across the road and just watch and wait.

I go to the pub and get a coffee while I think about it. I'm served by a youngish woman with black hair, blue eyes and an Irish accent.

I'm the only customer.

'Will you be wanting some breakfast?' she asks.

'You do breakfast?' Actually, I'm starving but was too excited to eat at Bunter's.

'Full English or something on toast.'

'Scrambled eggs on toast would be great, thanks.'

'You waiting for someone?' she smiles.

'No, I'm just a bit early for a meeting.'

A man's voice calls from behind the bar, 'Trish, have you got a minute?'

'I'm coming,' she smiles and goes back behind the bar.

Surely, it couldn't be, although she lives just across the road.

Within a few minutes she's back with the food.

'You're having a quiet morning?' I say, looking at the empty bar.

'Yes, it doesn't get busy 'til lunchtime. Then it goes mad.'

'I used to work in a bar,' I lie. 'Exhausting, isn't it! Then I had to look after my kids!'

'Me too,' she laughs. 'Luckily, they're in nursery until three.'

'Oh, how old are yours?'

'I'm a foster mum, so I get all ages, but at the moment, I've got a little boy aged 17 months and a girl of my own aged three.'

'You're a devil for punishment. You must really have your hands full!'

'Yes, but it pays well, and I'm a single mum, so…'

'Me too! But, of course, mine are grown up now. I miss having little ones around.'

'Maybe you'll have some grandchildren soon.'

'I really hope so.'

'Well, don't let your food get cold.'

'No...thanks.'

What are the chances? I can hardly believe it. She puts the kids in nursery all day and does another job. Not sure I like that. Surely, she's paid to be with them.

But if Gabriel is at the nursery, I might get a chance to see him. There can't be too many nurseries around here.

I have to play this very carefully. Trish will be here for the lunches and leave before three.

When she comes back for the dishes, I order another coffee.

'My kids used to go to the nursery in Church Road. Is that still there?' I ask.

'I've never heard of it. Was there one in Church Road?'

I didn't even know there was a Church Road, but there usually is in any town.

'Years ago. Where do you go, then?'

'Oakhill Drive. It used to be council offices, but the council moved into their new building two years ago, and it's now a nursery.'

'Any good?'

'Seems ok. You're local, then?' she asks.

'Used to be when my kids were small.'

Just then a group of people come in, and Trish excuses herself to serve them. I decide it's time to leave, giving Trish a friendly wave.

I walk away from the station and ask a passer-by where Oakhill Drive is. It's a ten-minute walk, apparently. Why is it when we ask for directions, we don't listen to the answer except for the first 'turn right at the post office' instruction?

I lose concentration after the first bit. Anyway, I turn right as instructed and then have to ask again.

Eventually, I find the nursery. I was hoping the children would be outside playing, but no such luck. It gives me shivers to think how near I am to my grandson. I think about what he's been through and want to cry, but I hold it together. He could have been living happily with me, but no, the bloody social workers know best. How dare they!

I walk up and down the street a couple of times, but there's no coffee bar or pub nearby. It's a mainly residential street, so I can't hang about looking suspicious.

It's 11.30am. I make my way back to the main street and wander aimlessly around the shops. Then I see a charity shop, and it gives me an idea. I look around until I see some children's clothes and toys in good condition including a little boy's jumper that looks new, and summer dresses that a little girl probably grew out of before she could wear them out.

I collect an armful of them and take them to the counter. I include a beautiful white teddy with a blue ribbon around its neck. On its tummy, it says, 'I love you'.

I don't go back to the nursery. I kill time until just after three and then go to the pub. I'm not supposed to know where Trish lives, so I tell the barman that I have something to deliver to her. He says fine, leave it here. Then I spot her out of the window just approaching her house.

'No worries,' I say. 'There she is!'

Chapter Nineteen

I casually walk across the street to her. She's struggling with a double buggy. She seems surprised but pleased to see a friendly face.

And there is my sweet boy.

I help her up the step into her cottage.

'I hope you won't be offended,' I say, 'but I went to see my daughter, who still lives in my old house, and I still have these which might come in handy. They're clean and as good as new. I know what it's like to be a single parent.' I hand her the bags from the charity shop.

She picks up the teddy and wells up. 'That's so kind of you. Come in.'

She unstraps the toddlers and lifts them out of the buggy. She then sits them at a little table and gives them both some pieces of cheese and sliced cucumber and carrot. Has my baby got enough teeth for that, I wonder?

'I'll put the kettle on,' she says. 'I'm Trish, by the way.'

Oh blimey, I can't say I'm Verity. She might have heard my name mentioned.

'I'm Jane,' I say.

'How did your meeting go?' she asks as she takes mugs from the cupboard.

Meeting? Ah yes, 'It was fine, thanks. How about you? You must be tired after your shift at the pub.'

'Oh, you get used to it. These are my monsters,' she says, smiling at the kids. 'My daughter is Eva, and the little boy is Gabriel.'

'They're gorgeous.'

I'm looking hard now to see who Gabriel is like. I can definitely see my side of the family in him. I wonder if Trish can hear my heart pounding.

'It must be hard to give up the children you foster?'

She hands me a mug of tea. 'Some more than others,' she admits. 'This little chap is a treasure.'

'How long will you have him for?'

'I don't know. They're looking for adoptive parents for him, but most people want newborns or girls.'

'But he's still a baby!'

'Yes, he might be okay. I'm sure they'll find someone. But there's so much red tape, it can take ages.'

'I'd adopt him! He's adorable,' I blurt.

'You could always try!' she laughs.

He starts to grizzle. 'Can I hold him?' I ask.

'Be my guest,' she smiles.

I gently pick him up, and I feel a lightning bolt of love surge through me. He smells right. Smells like my daughter. His soft blonde hair nuzzles against my face, and he snuggles into me.

'You've made a hit there!' says Trish.

I can't speak. Tears fall down my cheeks. I'm so tempted to tell this lovely lady that this is my child.

'Are you ok, Jane?'

'Sorry,' I sniffle, 'it just brings back so many memories of my own children. I never have contact with little ones these days.'

'You can always babysit for me,' she says.

'Really? Do you mean that? You don't know me.'

'Well, we're not supposed to without the social workers checking people out, but they drive you mad with all their rules. It would be nice to get out on my own occasionally.'

'I'll give you my number, and you think about it,' I say. 'If I can help you out and spend some time with little people again, it would be great.'

She grabs an old envelope and a pen, and I call my number out to her. Luckily, it's an easy number to remember.

I put Gabriel back in his chair and ruffle little Eva's hair.

'I'd better be off. Thank you so much for the tea. It's been a pleasure to meet you all.'

'And lovely to meet you, Jane,' says Trish. 'I'll definitely give you a call.'

As I sit on the train to Cambridge, I can hardly believe my luck, and I'm proud of myself for not snatching Gabriel and running!

Now, maybe I have an opportunity to see him on a regular basis. But supposing they find adoptive parents for him tomorrow?

Once he's adopted, I'll never find him unless, of course, Sally could be persuaded to do the business again. Sally, I need to pay her.

My heart aches. I so want Gabriel to be with me. But adoption checks are so thorough that I would never be accepted, and worse, I'd go to prison. Unless I could get a false identity, but they check with your friends and family, so it would be a mammoth job to involve lots of others if that were even possible.

I'm overwhelmed with anger at the system and with myself.

In a short train journey, I've gone from ecstatic to furious. But I held my grandson in my arms today, and I must be grateful for that.

I'm trying to think up a story to tell Zak about what I did today. But I needn't have worried. When I get back, he and Bunter are engrossed in a football match on TV, so they hardly notice me.

I go to our room and look out of the window at the park. People are going about their lives, children playing, dogs running about barking. Ordinary people with ordinary lives. How I envy them. How I wish I could turn the clock back.

I lie on the bed and think about the lovely man I married all those years ago. He was kind and caring and doted on Melody.

I think about the day she was born, arriving at 3am. She was a soft little bundle with a shock of black hair. Her little nose was squashed, and I was afraid she'd look like a boxer, but it soon looked normal, and she grew into a beautiful little girl.

Her hair changed from black to blonde as she grew up, and she turned heads wherever she went.

It broke James's heart when she took up with Chester. He tried to tell her that he was a bad lot, but it just drove a wedge between them. And the wedding day finished him off.

He would be horrified if he'd known what was to follow and the situation I find myself in now. If only I could speak to him.

Zak comes into the room looking elated. 'We won! I can't believe it. We're in with the big boys now!'

I give him a little smile.

'What's the matter with you?'

'Nothing. I'm fine.'

'Good, because we're going to go out and celebrate, you, me and Bunter.'

'You guys go out; you don't need me,'

'Verity, don't be a dead leg! We've booked a restaurant. Please? Will you be ready at seven?'

I give myself a kick up the backside. I realise I'm being a killjoy, and I have reason to celebrate too.

I give him a hug. 'I'll be ready,' I smile.

We have a couple of drinks before we go, so we're already pretty silly before we even get there. I'm trotting along in my heels which I never wear, and the boys are cracking jokes and swinging around lamp posts.

It's a happy feeling, a long-lost feeling of fun and freedom.

The restaurant is buzzing, and we have a fabulous meal and not a small amount of wine.

We talk about how much we love Cambridge and about football, of course!

Then Bunter drops a bombshell. We know he is a chef, but now he tells us that he's been offered a job in a gourmet pub not five minutes from my house. We're stunned. What happens now?

'I think I have the perfect solution,' says Bunter.

'Go on,' says a cautious Zak.

'Well, you're happy here in my house, so stay. And, Verity, maybe in return I could stay at yours? It's a five-minute walk from the pub and would save me all the commuting. Especially as I'll be working all hours.'

Zak and I look at each other.

'Look,' Bunter continues, 'Give it some thought. I start in two weeks.'

'Don't need to,' I say. 'You'd be most welcome to stay at my house.'

Zak nods, deep in thought.

'That's settled then! A bottle of your best champagne, please, waiter!'

'Our best champagne is a Bollinger, sir, at £120.'

'Ok, your worst champagne.'

'Your crappiest champagne,' laughs Zak.

'Your foul, revolting champagne,' I chip in.

'Your corked champagne,' says Bunter.

'Your recycled champagne,' splutters Zak as he starts laughing uncontrollably.

It's infectious, and we all join in until we can't breathe, and people are looking.

Bunter looks as if he's going to explode.

The waiter rushes off looking embarrassed.

Let's face it, we're all drunk.

The waiter returns and pours a small amount of something fizzy into Bunter's champagne flute. He composes himself and sips it with great reverence.

'Suitably foul,' he says. 'A vile little number from the north of the vineyard, I'd say.' Zak collapses again.

The waiter waits for instructions. 'Yes, go ahead man, pour.'

We finish off the bottle in no time. It's actually not bad, although we really don't care.

Eventually, we're the last ones in the restaurant. The table is a mess, and a solitary strawberry has fallen onto the tablecloth from my sundae.

That's when Bunter decides to sing.

'Let me take you there, cos I'm going to, strawberry fields, nothing is real, and nothing to get hung about, strawberry fields forever.'

Then Zak chimes in, 'Let me take you down cos I'm going to.'

And me... 'Strawberry fields...'

This gets louder and louder and to our amazement, the staff start to join in just when I thought we are going to get thrown out. It actually sounds pretty damn good. A sort of flash choir.

The owner comes over with a tea towel over his shoulder.

'You know what? It's great to see people really enjoying themselves and letting their hair down. We tend to get a lot of stuffed shirts in here. But I didn't say that! And we're all Beatles lovers here.'

Bunter says, 'I hate the Beatles,' and we're all off again.

'I hope you're not driving,' says the owner, who has introduced himself as Sebastian. 'Where do you live?'

And Bunter's off again, 'We all live in a yellow submarine,' he wails.

Somehow, Sebastian manages to guide us all to the door, and we're on the street. We're not the only ones. The football match must have been a big deal because there are football fans singing and shouting. But it's all good-humoured until, suddenly, out of nowhere, a fight breaks out.

Fists are flying, and a crowd gathers. Then there's teeth and blood, and before I can stop him, Zak steps in.

I try to pull him back, but he's in the zone. Bunter knows his own size and his limits and stands back.

Instead of the fight breaking up, it escalates with more people joining in. And they're not messing about. Zak is trying to pull people off each other, but he's outnumbered. Not to mention drunk.

Within minutes, the police arrive in numbers, and then an ambulance. They grab and arrest everyone in the centre of the melee, including Zak!

I run up to the officer, 'He was just trying to stop them!' I shout.

'You with him?'

'Yes.'

'Ok, you're nicked too.'

'What for?'

'Obstructing a police officer.'

'I didn't.'

But it's no good. We're put in the back of a police van, and Zak is even handcuffed.

I look back at Bunter. He's struggling to stay upright and leaning on Sebastian who has come to see what all the fuss is about.

It's surprising how quickly you can sober up when you're having your fingerprints taken and even your DNA.

We're put in separate cells, and I can hear Zak snoring, as well as shouting from others that were arrested for fighting.

How can he go to sleep? This could be it for us. My mind whirs from one disaster to the next. The bank robbery, the demise of Chester, the gold bar, the celebrity in the swimming pool, my poor Brad, the diamonds...

Calm down, Verity. Think logically. Oh my God, Zak is supposed to be dead! He's at the undertakers in the Isle of Wight or maybe buried by now. How will he explain that? I hope he doesn't have Brad's ID on him.

Sometime in the early morning, I'm asked if I want a solicitor. Do I need one? I don't know. I say yes, just in case.

Much later, I'm given a breakfast of beans on toast and a polystyrene cup of tea.

I'm still dressed for an evening out and have had to leave my high heels outside in case I impale myself with them.

Eventually, I hear the key in the door, and I'm taken to an interview room where I'm introduced to Maria, who is a solicitor. I explain that I didn't do anything except try to get Zak to keep out of it.

221

'Normally,' she says, 'I'd advise my clients to give a no comment interview, but in your case, I would just go ahead and tell them what you've told me.'

'But they said I was obstructing the police!'

'Yes, well, they would, wouldn't they? Let's see what they have to say.'

Of course, Maria knows nothing of our backgrounds, so I'm still worried.

Maria leaves the room. Then I overhear a conversion in the corridor. Male voices.

'Are you talking about Verity Anne Brown?'

'Yes, she was involved in a breach of the peace last night. Hertfordshire says there was a lot of suspicion, but nothing concrete, so she's not wanted. They were more interested in her associate Zak Bently.'

'Who's the guy she was with last night?'

'Well, that's the strange thing. We don't have Bently's fingerprints, but we do have a mugshot of him, and he looks like this guy. But he was reported dead in the Isle of Wight months ago.'

'Who does he say he is?'

At this moment, Maria returns with a policewoman, and I can't hear any more.

Then, a policeman in plain clothes comes in and switches on a tape recorder.

'Interview commencing 11.20am with DC James and…'

'Maria Mathews.'

'P.C. Atkinson.'

'And…' he looks at me, 'say your name,'

'Um, Verity Brown.'

'Right, Verity, tell us what happened last night.'

I realise that I was calling Zak by his name in front of the police last night. Now what do I call him?

I look at the solicitor, and say, 'No comment.'

She looks bewildered.

D.C James continues, 'You told the officer last night that you were trying to stop the man you were with from getting involved with a fight. Is that right?'

'No comment.'

'What is the name of the man you were with?'

'No comment.'

'You called him Zak.'

'No comment.'

'You used to associate with Zak Bently. Where is he now?'

'No comment.'

'Is Zak Bently the man you were with?'

'No comment.'

'Did Zak die in the Isle of Wight?'

'No comment.'

'Interview concluded at 11.23 am.'

The officers get up and leave, leaving me with Maria. She gives me a puzzled look and then leaves the room.

Ten minutes later, I'm told I can go. No charges. Free to go.

Chapter Twenty

I get a cab back to Bunter's. He's in the kitchen nursing a hangover over a mug of coffee and some pain killers.

'Oh, sweetheart, are you ok?' he says.

'I could use a coffee.'

He stands up gingerly and pours me a coffee.

'Where's Zak?'

'Still at the nick.'

'Are they charging him with anything?'

'I don't know. They didn't tell me anything.'

'Have they charged you?'

'No.'

'I should think not. Can't believe they arrested you.'

We drink our coffee.

After a minute or two Bunter says, 'I'll ring the police and ask them what the score is with Zak.'

'NO! No, don't do that…' I can't let him say the name Zak to the police.

'Ok, you're probably right. They might not tell me anything anyway. We'll just have to wait.'

I go to our room to have a shower, catch up on some sleep and have a think.

I had convinced myself that due to all our misdemeanours, I would go to jail for a long time if I came into contact with the authorities. But could it be that I'm now home free?

It's been put to the test, and now I don't have to look over my shoulder anymore or keep running, unless, of course, Zak is found out and takes me down with him. I know he wouldn't do that deliberately, but the circumstantial evidence could mount up.

I don't know how to find out what's happening to him without using his name.

I sleep until my phone rings at 4.05pm. I grab it quick.

'Zak?'

'Sorry, is that Jane?' says a woman's voice.

Must be a wrong... oh, Jane... 'Yes, it's Jane, is that Trish?'

'Yes, hi, sorry to bother you.'

'No, it's ok. I was just snoozing, so not quite with it. How are you?'

'Good, thanks, but my mum's ill. I want to go and see her, but she lives a good two hours away, and I can manage Eva on the train and buses, and Mum wants to see her, but with two toddlers, it would be a nightmare,' she gabbled. 'I wondered if you could have Gabriel for the day. He seemed to take a shine to you.'

I sit bolt upright.

'Yes, I'd be delighted. When did you want to go?'

'As soon as possible. Tomorrow, if you could make it?'

There's still no news about Zak as I sit on the train to see Gabriel.

It's been two days now. Have they taken him to prison? Is he still at the police station?

Bunter is staying in to make sure that he's there if Zak comes back.

When I get to Station Terrace, Trish is at the door waiting for me.

'Jane! I'm so glad you're on time. The trains often run late, and mine is due in seven minutes, so you don't mind if I dash, do you?'

Without waiting for an answer, she dashes off with Eva running alongside her as fast as her little legs will carry her.

I find Gabriel sitting happily in a highchair sucking a rusk. I have him all to myself for a whole day.

I look at him and see Melody. Tears sting behind my eyes. My daughter is missing her beautiful son growing up, and this gorgeous child is being pushed from pillar to post with no mum or dad.

I gently take him from the highchair and give him a long hug. He snuggles into me. It feels so right.

I put him in the playpen with some toys and make myself a cup of tea. Then, I sit down and watch him play, drinking in everything about him.

I want to take pictures of him and selfies with him in my arms, but my burner phone can only make calls and texts. I must get a camera.

As I inspect my phone, I get a text.

It's Zak. 'I'm home. Where are you?'

I'm overwhelmed with relief.

'Thank God. Are you ok?'

'Yes, fine, where are you?'

'Visiting friends. Be back about six.'

227

'Can't you get back before that?'

'Sorry, hun, I'll explain later. I'll bring a takeaway. Let me know what you want.'

It's 5pm, and I need to get back to Cambridge and Zak.

I get a text, 'Sorry, Jane, my mum's very sick. I can't leave her. Please, could you hang on until tomorrow?'

'Sorry to hear that, Trish, but I need to get home. I'll take Gabriel with me.'

I find some carrier bags and pack some nappies and baby food and load them and my grandson into the buggy, which is big and cumbersome.

The timing is perfect as a train arrives just as we get to the station. It's a struggle with the bags and the pushchair, and the train is crowded, but a young guy helps me, and we manage to get the pushchair folded, and a woman gives up her seat for me. So many kind people. I text Zak and ask him to meet me at the station.

But then Gabriel starts to cry, and I don't have anything to give him. No dummy, no bottle. I give him my phone, and that does the trick, to the relief of everyone around us.

Zak's face as we get off the train is a picture. He helps me with the pushchair.

'What the...who's this?'

'I'm babysitting. My friend's mum is ill, and she had to take off. It was the least I could do.'

'You're too soft.'

'We all need a bit of help sometimes.'

228

'That's why I love you,' he says as he kisses my cheek. 'Here, give me the little fella. What's his name?'

Oh, hell. I can't say Gabriel. He knows that's my grandson's name.

'It's Tom.'

'Hello, Tom. He's a cute little chap, isn't he!'

'You don't think Bunter will mind, do you?'

'No, he loves kids. He's a big kid himself. How long have you got him for?'

'Probably only until tomorrow.'

Bunter is bored and delighted with the new arrival. He's a natural and soon has 'Tom' giggling. He takes charge while I catch up with Zak in the kitchen.

'So?' I ask, dying to know what happened with the police.

'Well, they're not stupid. They pretty much know what happened with the bank robbery and with Chester, but it's all circumstantial. They tried to convince me that they had all the evidence they needed to charge me, but I didn't say a word the whole time I was in there. They gave me the third degree about the Isle of Wight, and how come my ID was on the body? Again, no evidence. They even brought in the undertaker to ask if he recognised me, but he couldn't be sure.'

'So, how has it been left?'

'I'm on police bail "pending further enquiries".'

'Do they know you're staying here?'

'I didn't tell them, but I guess they could have followed me.'

'You need to get rid of Brad's police ID.'

'Don't worry, I did that ages ago.'

'Maybe we need to move on.'

'My thoughts exactly.'

Bunter is in the doorway with Tom in his arms.

'You planning to skip bail?' he asks.

I look at Zak.

'It's ok. I've told him everything.'

'Everything?'

'Yes. I trust him with my life.'

'And my life!'

Bunter puts his arm around me. 'Sweetheart, I will do anything I can to help. You've nothing to fear from me.'

'Ok, well, since everything's out in the open, this little boy is Gabriel, my grandson.'

Zak's mouth drops open. 'What? How?'

'I traced his foster carer, and she let me babysit.'

'Does she know who you are?' asks an incredulous Zak.

'No.'

'For Christ's sake!'

'He's my grandson!' I yell, 'I have a right!'

'Come on,' says Bunter, 'Let's sit down and talk about this.' We all go into the sitting room.

There's a knock at the door. Bunter goes to answer it, and two minutes later, the place is knee deep in cops. They have a warrant to search the place.

I clutch Gabriel to me. Both Bunter and Zak are as cool as cucumbers.

An hour later, having turned the place upside down and finding nothing to interest them, they leave. I'm trembling. Bunter pours us all a drink and clinks glasses with Zak.

'To our wonderful boys in blue,' he says. 'Better luck next time!'

As we eat breakfast the next day, my phone goes.

'Jane, it's Trish. Is everything alright?'

'Yes, fine. What's happening?'

'Jane… my mum died last night.' There's a sob, and for a minute, Trish can't speak.

'I'm so sorry, Trish. Are you okay?'

'Yes, sorry, it's just I'll have to stay here to sort things out. I'm going to have to tell social services to take Gabriel back. I can't cope with both kids at the moment. Can they pick him up from you, or could you take him to their offices? I'll have to say that I've only just left him with you as it was an emergency or else they won't let me foster again.'

Gabriel is on my lap, grinning at something daft that Zak is doing.

She wants me to pass my baby on to some stranger as if he's a parcel so they can pass him on to someone else?

'Trish, I can look after him.'

'I know, and it's good of you, but it's not allowed. I could get into serious trouble as it is.'

'Ok, look, leave it to me. You've got enough on your plate,' I say. 'I'll ring them and say that your mum has died, and you've left him with me as I'm your best friend. And I can make arrangements directly with them. Okay?'

'You're a lifesaver, thanks.'

'No problem, and if I were you, I'd switch off my phone so they can't give you any hassle! You know what these jobsworths can be like!'

'I do. I get sick of all their fussing. I *will* switch the phone off, thanks.'

'Do they have your mum's number?'

'No, I don't think so, but I'll switch it off anyway. She won't be needing it.' More sobbing.

Ten minutes later, I send her a text:

'Social Services send their condolences and say that's fine. They're on their way to pick Gabriel up now. They will contact you again in a month or two to see how you're doing. Hope you're ok. Don't worry, all sorted this end.'

Zak is watching me. 'What are you doing? You're going to give Gabriel back to social services?'

'No, I'm going to call Fedex and see how many times they can play pass the parcel with him.'

'Jeez, Verity…'

'Look, social services won't know for ages. As far as they know, he's happily settled with Trish.'

'They probably do regular inspections,' says Bunter quietly.

'Maybe, but Trish has been fostering for years, so I doubt if they'd bother her very often. They're busy people.'

Bunter doesn't give up, 'Verity, when they do find out, every cop in the land will be looking for you, and it will be all over the papers.'

'And how ridiculous is that! Loving gran looks after her own grandchild! The lunatics are running the asylum!'

Zak chimes in, 'Look, you have no criminal record... yet, anyway! The social services are still looking for adoptive parents for Gabriel. Why not go the official route and apply to adopt him?'

'Because if they say no, I'm screwed, and I'll never see him again.'

Bunter is pacing up and down. He's become very attached to Gabriel.

'Look,' he says, 'my friend Adam is a solicitor. How about I ring him and ask for his advice?'

'Wouldn't he have to be a family solicitor? He might just do conveyancing or crime,' says Zak.

'I'm not sure what he does, but there's no harm in asking. If he doesn't know, he's bound to know someone who does.'

I don't think I'm ready to trust a stranger. It's just too important. And a lengthy legal battle could get expensive.

Gabriel has gone to sleep on my lap, and his little hand is gripping my thumb.

I'm so overwhelmed with love for him that I'm ready to kill anyone who tries to take him from me. My flesh and blood. It's nobody's business but mine. To hell with lawyers and social workers. Nobody could love this child as I do. I gave birth to his mother, and I will care for him as I cared for her.

Zak and Bunter have been talking, but I haven't heard any of it. I feel panicked now. Under threat. I want to get away.

'What do you think, Verity?' asks Zak.

'Think about what?'

'Have you not heard a word we've said?'

'No, sorry, what did you say?' Zak sighs, and Bunter looks at his feet.

'We think you should see the solicitor ASAP.'

'No. From today, Gabriel is called Tom, and we need to move on.'

Bunter chips in, 'Am I right in thinking that this Trish woman has your details?'

'No, she only knows me as Jane and has my burner phone number, and I've already chucked that.'

The next day, Bunter goes to his new job and to live in my house. Zak and I take Tom and catch a train heading for Stansted Airport.

We can't take Tom abroad without a passport, but we can fly to Northern Ireland, so that's what we do.

We arrive in Belfast in the late afternoon and go to McDonalds for a burger.

We then book into a cheap hotel and get on the phone to lettings agents to see if we can rent a flat.

There's no shortage, and we get an appointment to view a furnished two bed flat at £750 a month.

It has to be cheaper than staying in hotels, even if we don't stay for long.

This is my first visit to Belfast, and I don't know what I was expecting, but I'm pleasantly surprised. I suppose all I'd heard about Northern Ireland in the past had been about the troubles, so maybe I'd been expecting a bit of a bomb site. But here I am looking at beautiful buildings and a stunning waterfront.

It's fun to explore new places, and once again, we become tourists for a couple of weeks.

The first flat we view is fine. Basic, but ok.

Our little fella is toddling about getting into mischief. This feels like a real family now. But I still feel unsafe. We need to disguise ourselves somehow.

Over breakfast I suggest, 'If and when they look for Gabriel, they'll be looking for a boy, right?'

'Well, duh!'

'So, why don't we dress him as a girl and change his name?'

'Poor little sod! You can't do that. He won't know what he is.'

'He won't remember this part of his life. It'll make him safer.'

'Firstly, he's Gabriel, then Tom, then Gabriel again. Now what? Arabella?'

'Zak, I'm serious. They're looking for a boy.'

'They're also looking for us, and *we* can't change sex overnight.'

'I don't know. It could be fun! I could put my hair in a cap and smoke a pipe, and you could get some dresses from a charity shop and buy a wig. Or you could get a burka!'

'Yes, very funny. You are a total nutter!'

We've been here for a month now, and the novelty has worn off. We have nothing to do all day except the usual household chores and shopping.

Gabriel is a happy little soul and very little trouble. But we don't know what to do next. Zak is getting irritable, and I'm not much better.

We both got rid of our old burner phones and now only have one. The only person who has the number is Bunter because he's living in my house.

When it rings early one morning, it has to be him.

'Bunter!' I'm glad of a distraction.

'Hi, Verity. You ok? Can I talk to Zak, please?'

I pass the phone to Zak, disappointed that he doesn't want to chat with me. Zak listens for a minute and then wanders outside, out of earshot.

What are those two up to? I try to eavesdrop but with no luck.

Minutes later, Zak returns, looking serious.

'What?' I ask.

'Sit down.'

'What? You're scaring me.'

'A social worker went to your house and spoke to Bunter. She had contacted Trish, and, of course, Trish was horrified to find out that Gabriel hadn't been returned.'

'And?'

'After Trish described what happened, the police checked the station CCTV, and there you were with Gabriel. One of the social workers recognised you.'

'So, now what?'

'The best of it is, and you're not going to like this… Gabriel is not your grandson.'

'Of course, he is. What do you mean?'

'Your Gabriel was adopted, which is what you were told originally. The cleaner who gave you the info about the foster mum got the wrong Gabriel. Apparently, it's a fashionable name at the moment.'

'Don't fall for that! They just want me to bring him back.'

'No, Verity. It's true. They can prove it with DNA.'

'Well, I don't believe it.'

'They've said they'll send you photos every year of your Gabriel and when he's eighteen.'

'When he's eighteen! No, I'm not giving him up. It's just a trick,' I say as I pick up the little boy I've come to love.

Zak puts his arm around me, 'Sweetheart, this little chap is not yours.'

'Well, even if he isn't, he's just going to go to a foster home and then…'

The tears flow, an avalanche of pent-up misery, fear and disappointment.

'Maybe I could adopt him,' I wail.

'Honey, as far as the authorities are concerned, we kidnapped a child who is unrelated to us. I don't think adoption is likely.'

It's three days before I get over the shock and accept the inevitable. Gabriel has to go back.

It seems crazy. He has a perfectly good home with us, but now he has to be passed around due to stupid laws and red tape.

I feel as though I'm losing my Gabriel all over again.

We fly back to England and take our poor little guy back to Trish's house. She's probably been barred from fostering, but she'll know who to take him to. I leave him in his buggy on her doorstep and phone her to say he's outside. I watch from the pub window as she comes out, looks around and takes him in.

I throw my burner phone in the bin after taking the battery out.

Chapter Twenty-One

We decide to risk staying at Bunter's place in Cambridge while we decide on our next move and get over the heartbreaking events of the day.

In the morning, we realise we need to take stock, and I go to Google for some answers.

I look up the soap star that I still have on my conscience. There are several items about her death. But this one is the most interesting:

At the inquest of soap star Georgia Vincent, the coroner reported that she had died from a heart-stopping cocktail of illegal drugs. The report showed that she would have died whether or not she had been in the water.

So, I didn't kill her! Thank God. Why do celebrities who appear to have everything take dangerous drugs? I'll never understand it.

Zak is laid back and watching daytime TV while scoffing toast.

I Google Chester.

Body in the woods thought to be a gangland murder. Chester Robinson, known to be a violent man who mixed with criminals, was found in a shallow grave with some of the money from a bank robbery beside him.

This has baffled police, whose spokesman said, 'It seems strange that anyone would leave money with him, but it could have been to tie him in with the bank robbery. Enquiries are ongoing.'

I can't help thinking that if there was any evidence against us, it would have been found by now.

I look up the bank robbery. Isn't Google amazing!

The Covent Garden Branch of the HSBC bank was robbed yesterday, etc.

Then:

Two men have been arrested in connection with the HSBC bank robbery in Covent Garden. Tony Willis and Scott Barnes have been remanded in custody while enquiries continue.

Wow, so Tony and Scott have been caught! Yippee.

Next, I Google poor Brad:

A missing police officer's body was delivered to an undertaker in the Isle of Wight by a bogus policeman, according to Hampshire police.

The body carried the ID of another man, but the suspicious undertaker immediately contacted the police and extensive enquiries have shown that the body is that of Bradley Benson, a Met police inspector who was working in the area.

A post-mortem showed that the officer had died from a blow to the head.

The owner of the ID has been interviewed and bailed pending further inquiries.

Zak was an idiot to think that swapping IDs would work. Fancy leaving his own ID! It looks so bad on him, but it was a genuine accident.

But it scares me. If they think Zak killed one of their own, they will pull out all the stops. But thinking logically, I was the only witness, although

240

Rip was soon involved. Poor innocent Rip. I wonder how he is.

After a fight, I'm sure Zac's DNA would be all over Brad. But surely that's not proof of murder on its own? I wish I knew more about how the police work.

This has all made me twitchy, and I'm keen to get moving again.

After updating Zak, he seems to relish the drama, and his old perky self-returns.

He swings me around the room. 'Where have you always wanted to go?' he smiles. 'We can go anywhere. The world's our lobster. You name it, we'll go there.'

Well, put like that…

He continues, 'The Bahamas, Outer Mongolia, Bognor, The Seychelles, Dimchurch… where?'

'Okay… um…'

I can't help thinking, here we go again, but it's also an adventure where I have the man I love to myself.

Maybe we could get a live-in job somewhere. Our money won't last forever, and we need something to do. I start flicking through the ads. There are couples wanted to do housekeeping and gardening, but that doesn't appeal.

Then I see an ad for staff on a cruise ship. Now that's more like it.

They want bar staff, cleaners, chefs, entertainers, lecturers, tour guides…all sorts of people. There must be something we could do.

'Zak.'

'Yes?' Zak answers lazily as he channel hops.

'How do you fancy working on a cruise ship?'

'Working?' he looks horrified.

'Yeah, you know, doing stuff and getting paid for it.'

'I fancy going on a cruise.'

'Good, well that's a start.'

'But not working.'

'Why not? It'd be fun, and we need something to do. A cruise would only last for a week or two. If we got jobs on a cruise ship, we could stay for months or even years.'

'We're too old.'

'Too old for what?'

'Manual labour.'

I can't help laughing. He's as fit as a flea and very strong, while I'm unfit and could do with losing a few pounds.

'Can you dance?' I ask.

'Nope, why?'

'They want someone to dance with the single ladies.'

'They'll all be over seventy.'

'So?'

'What else have they got?'

'Oh, here's one for you; they want someone to give talks on embroidery and knitting.'

'Perfect!' He jumps to his feet and stands tall as if addressing a large audience.

'Good morning, Ladeez. I have been knitting and embroidering since I was in nappies, so I'm sure you'll pick it up easily.

'In fact (he indicates the rugby shirt he's wearing), I knitted this myself and embroidered the

242

logo. You have to be careful not to stab yourself, or your model if you use one. I once used a blow-up doll as my model for a bikini top I was sewing and accidentally stabbed her with my needle. It didn't go down well. Well, actually it did go down very well…'

'You idiot!' I laugh. It's good to see the old Zak back again.

I give him a hug, and we both fall onto the sofa. The next bit is X rated so go and watch TV or get yourself a cup of tea. No, go on, butt out, this is private. You won't be getting fifty shades of anything here.

Today we're going to London to the offices of a cruise line. They seem to need a lot of people, so we're hoping the personal approach might work.

I told Zak to bring his knitting, ha ha!

We're in good spirits and smartly dressed. We manage to talk our way into the HR department and are given forms to fill in.

How many languages do you speak? Um, still having trouble with English.

Have you ever been on a cruise ship? No.

What is your experience in hospitality? Zilch.

Do you have a valid UK passport? Yes (Phew).

This goes on for a few pages. Then they want to see our CVs. We don't have CVs.

We are asked into an interview room where a tired-looking man of about sixty looks at us over his glasses.

'What can you do?' he asks.

'We can turn our hands to most things,' I say with a smile.

'Like what?'

'Bar work,' says Zak, 'or …'

'Admin, or reception…'

'Do you have bar experience?'

'Yes,' lies Zak. This side of the bar!

'What are you doing at the moment?'

'Well,' says Zak with confidence,' I've just come out of the army, and Verity has been looking after the house and children. Now we're free and looking for a new lifestyle.'

'References?'

'Of course, we can get those to you by tomorrow,' Zak smiles.

The guy gives us a long look.

'You're probably aware from our ads that we need staff urgently. This is because we have ships leaving this week. Forgive me for saying so, but we normally take on younger people, but with this short notice, it might not be a bad thing to take people with life experience. How soon could you travel?'

'We're totally free,' I say.

'Ok, we'll give you a trial for one cruise. You'll need to go to our Southampton office tomorrow, and they'll take it from there.'

He passes us some paperwork which explains the clothes we'll need and the salary details as well as lots of rules and regulations.

We come away feeling exhausted and not a little bit shocked.

The ship looks more like a block of flats. It's enormous.

I'm as excited as a kid as we board. We're directed to an office where we're given our room key and told to report back when we've settled in to have our duties explained to us. We don't even know what our jobs are yet.

Our room is windowless and tiny. There are twin beds, a desk, a wardrobe and a tiny bathroom. Apparently, we're lucky not to share with strangers. A lot of the crew cabins have bunk beds for four or even six people.

But it's ok. We won't be spending much time in here.

We make our way back to the office. The ship is amazing. Everything is luxurious. There are bars and restaurants, theatres and pools, shops and gyms. I'm getting nervous now. What will we be doing?

In the office, we meet Thelma, who is about our age. She's friendly and kind and has been cruising for twenty-two years.

We have a little chat, and she realises that we are totally green. She suggests bar work for Zak and asks me if I would prefer housekeeping or laundry! My face must have been saying sod off because she looks back at her list and back at me.

'I don't suppose you're any good at photography?' she asks.

I am, as it happens.

'I did a course at my local college a few years ago,' I say proudly.

'Our photographer sadly passed away recently, and so all his equipment is here. My understanding is that with digital photography, there's not much to it. Just point the camera and shoot!' she laughs. 'Then you print out the picture and display them on boards for customers to buy.'

I'm sure it's not as easy as that.

'Do you want to give that a bash?' she asks.

I can't believe this. There must be dozens of professional photographers who would give their right arms for this job. What if I make a hash of it, cut people's heads off? Zak looks as astonished as I do.

The woman sits back in her chair.

'Look,' she continues, 'the ship leaves tomorrow. We have no photographer. Most people like a picture of themselves dressed up or meeting the captain. They take pictures themselves, but they like one mounted in a frame with the ship's name on it. There's a girl who does all that, so you would just need to take the pics. If they're no good, don't use them, but I'm sure we can all manage to get some decent shots. And you've been on a course. What do you say?'

'Ok, it could be fun!'

'And a great way to meet people,' she adds.

There is a bewildering array of equipment in the photographer's room, cameras, interchangeable lenses, tripods, printers, light measuring thingies.

There are pictures on the walls of previous cruises, which is helpful as it gives me an idea of what's needed. There are mainly formal groups in their finery, but also some casual shots in locations all over the ship.

Luckily, there's also a computer with internet access, so I can look up anything I don't know about the cameras. This is some learning curve.

My helper is Ellie, an unassuming girl of about nineteen. She has already done four cruises so knows the ropes.

I choose an impressive-looking camera which has an 'easy' setting for idiots. I feel quite important. It's better than changing sheets or working in the laundry. I can't believe my luck. I think Zak's quite jealous, but then he has constant access to alcohol, so he'll be happy enough. He wasn't so thrilled to learn that he has to wear a uniform!

My first job is to take pictures of passengers as they arrive. Many are nervous and don't know what to expect, so they're not expecting too much of me. I snap away happily, but surprisingly, it's quite exhausting.

When I go back to my office and check the results, I'm pleasantly surprised...mostly.

Zak pops in to see how I'm doing. We look through the pics together. I think he's quite impressed.

'You jammy sod,' he smiles, 'you've really fallen on your feet!' He gives me a hug.

And then, he stops scrolling.

'Oh my God, no!'

'What?'

'You know who that is?'

I take a closer look. 'No... who?'

Chapter Twenty-Two

'It's the bloody bank manager, Collins!'

'Are you sure?'

'Of course, I'm sure. I'll never forget his face. Sometimes I see his scared face in my dreams, poor sod.'

'He's not likely to recognise you, surely.'

'Why not? He saw my face when he handed me the money.'

'It's a big ship; there's over a thousand people.'

'But I work behind a bar. He's bound to buy a drink at some point.'

'There must be a dozen bars…'

'Ok, you're right. I'll stop panicking. It was just a shock seeing him again. Trouble is there's no escape from a ship once we're at sea.'

Right on cue, the ship sails out of the harbour. We make our way to the decks which are lined with people waving to those left behind as if they were emigrating, not on a two-week holiday.

'Was he on his own?' asks Zak.

'I don't know. I doubt it.'

'We'll have to have another look through the photos to see who he's near.'

'Ok, but don't worry for now. Let's try to enjoy this trip.'

It's not like Zak to panic about anything. That's usually my job. And believe me, I'm panicking. But I need to keep Zak calm.

I go back to my office and look carefully through all the pictures. Ellie has already started to mount them, ready for sale.

I find Mr Collins, with his comb over and thin specs, but he was boarding alongside several others, and there's no way of telling if he was with any of them. There is a middle-aged woman near him who could be a possibility, so I make a mental note.

There are three large boards outside the office where all the pictures are displayed. Ellie deals with all of that.

Zak has to work ridiculous hours; well, we both do, so by the time we get to bed, we're exhausted.

He says he's enjoying it, although he's having to learn to make cocktails. He's a gregarious person and enjoys the company of the other bar staff and the customers.

I'm surprised to learn that we don't get any days off, so it's relentless. Fine if you're twenty, but jeez, it's hard when you're, well, a bit older.

Today we're in the Bay of Biscay, and the ship is bobbing about like a cork. One good thing about my job is that I can disappear if I need to for a few minutes here or there unless there is a formal night or something special happening.

And I need to go on deck right now and look at the horizon. That's what they tell you to do if you feel a bit seasick. The bad thing is that the passengers soon get to know the ship's photographer, so it's hard to hide.

As soon as I feel better, I make my way back to work, looking in on Zak on the way. I just pop my head around the door, and he gives me a little smile. The bar is fairly quiet, and he looks quite relaxed.

I love that man.

When I get back to the office, my boss, Thelma, is there. She's looking at the pictures and chatting to Ellie. She turns to me.

'How's it going?'

'Fine, I think,'

'You're looking a bit green around the gills. Are you OK?'

'Yes, thanks, just not got my sea legs yet.'

'The Bay of Biscay is often like this. We'll be in calmer waters soon.'

'That's good. Um, I just wander around the ship taking pictures, but are there any special areas or events you want me to cover?'

'Well, people who get invited to the captain's table often like evidence of it!' she laughs. 'And tomorrow night there'll be a formal dinner, so you'll need to photograph each person or couple as they enter. Most people buy that picture.'

'Thanks. That's very helpful.'

'Anytime. You know where I am. How's Zak doing?'

'Fine, thanks, he's loving it, but the long hours take some getting used to.'

'You'd be surprised how quickly he'll adapt. Let me know if either of you need anything.'

With that, she's gone.

It's the night of the formal dinner, and I put on my one and only long frock. I'm the wrong shape for

251

it, but it's the best I can do. But I'll be on my feet all night, so I can't wear heels. I have to wear flat shoes, so I do not look glamorous!

I arrive early to get set up with my tripod. These pictures need to look professional and not like snaps. There is even an area set aside with a curtain backdrop just for this purpose.

Soon people start to arrive and wow! The women are wearing the most fabulous dresses and dripping with jewellery. The men look equally splendid. For some, this is a huge moment that they have prepared for for months. For others, it's just another black-tie dinner.

The lighting's good, so this is the easiest job. Everyone wants their picture taken, and they're happy to pose. I don't even need to take their names, as the pictures are simply displayed, and they buy them if they want them.

They're queuing up now and don't seem to mind waiting while others take their turn.

Then, right in front of me is Mr Collins and presumably Mrs Collins.

He's a quiet man, but she chatters away and seems really pleasant. She's a large lady, and her blue satin dress is struggling to contain her.

When everyone is seated, I do my rounds of the restaurant. It seems intrusive to photograph people when they're eating but most don't seem to mind.

I then go to the captain's table, and there are Mr and Mrs Collins!

I wonder what you have to do to qualify to sit at the captain's table.

There are eight people on that circular table, and they all look up and smile. One or two try to make a little bit of polite conversation with me. The captain says something, but he's not English, and I can't understand him. I smile and just keep snapping.

Then Mrs Collins says, 'My husband loves photography, don't you, love. Maybe we could buy you a drink and pick your brains about a few things one day?'

I'm flummoxed. 'That's very kind of you, but it's difficult... I'm working.'

To my horror, the captain joins in, and this time, I understand him despite his Polish accent.

'I'm sure we could spare you for an hour during the trip,' he smiles.

'Um, that's kind, well, thanks. I'm sure we can arrange something...'

And with that, I leave as fast as I can.

When I get back to our cabin, I tell Zak about it.

'Jeez, can't we go anywhere without someone popping up out of the woodwork to throw a spanner in the works? Do they know you're with someone?'

'It wasn't mentioned.'

'Well, let's hope they'll get distracted and forget about it. We'll be in Lisbon tomorrow, so they'll probably disembark for the day.'

Unfortunately, there's no disembarking for us. There's too much work to do.

Zak has to be behind the bar for those who stay on board, and I have a lot of printing to do.

Luckily, we don't see anything of the Collinses.

Today is another day at sea. I get to my office at 9am and already, passengers are perusing the photos on display. Ellie is happily taking orders...from Mrs Collins!

Mr Collins can't be far away. I quickly text Zak, *'Stay away, Mrs C here.'*

He quickly replies, *'What, why?'*

'Just ordering pics, but he must be nearby.'

'OK, be careful.'

I try to avoid her, but she sees me.

'Hello, dear. Good to see you again. We love our photos, don't we, love? Oh, he's disappeared again.'

'Oh, glad you like them,' I say, trying to look busy.

'Oh yes, as I say, Ken is a keen photographer. He'd love you to join us for dinner so he could pick your brains.'

'Well, that would be lovely, but I'm afraid we're not allowed to eat with the guests.'

'Oh really? The captain seemed to think it would be ok. Well, maybe just a drink at the Ocean Bar? We're going there for a drink before lunch.' The Ocean Bar is where Zak is working.

'Um, what time will you be in there?'

'About twelve, say you'll join us!'

'Thanks, I will if I can get away,' I smile.

I walk into the office and leave her talking to Ellie.

I get straight on the phone to warn Zak.

'They'll be in your bar at twelve.'

'Shit, this is a nightmare. I can't just leave the bar.'

'Won't there be others on duty?'

254

'Yes, but it's a busy time.'

'Say you've got the runs and disappear for an hour.'

'Can't do that every day.'

'Ok, well, I'll join them and try to distract them. If you see him making for the bar, go to the loo or something. I'll try to persuade them that another bar is better.'

I get to the bar with my camera just before twelve. It's filling up fast, and I wander about taking pictures. When I see the Collinses arrive, I guide them to a far corner of the bar. I glance at Zak. He's watching us like a hawk.

Mr Collins takes out his wallet and asks what I'd like to drink. I tell him to put his money away...I get a staff discount. But he insists. He walks towards the bar, and Zak almost knocks another bar man over as he makes for the exit.

But there is a queue at the bar, so Ken Collins has a short wait.

Minutes later, I get a text.

'Can I come out now?'

'No. I'll let you know.'

'Sorry about that,' I say to Mrs Collins. 'We have to be on call at all times.'

'Yes, I can see it's a full-time job,' she says.

Eventually, Mr Collins returns with the drinks. There are quite a few people standing about blocking our view from the bar, so I text Zak, '*OK.*'

He comes back to an angry-looking barman who has been managing on his own. Zak looks apologetic and holds his stomach.

So, then I get the Spanish inquisition from Ken Collins. Good job I went on a photographic course, or I'd really be in trouble. He seems satisfied with my answers.

I then ask them about their lives.

He tells me he's retired from his job as a bank manager.

His wife chimes in, 'He retired early after an incident at the bank. He hasn't been the same since.'

'An incident?'

'Yes, it was awful. The bank was robbed. Tell her, dear....he was kidnapped and everything.'

'Well,' he says, with a face that says not this again, 'I was kidnapped, and my wife was held captive by some thugs. They kept me in some industrial place overnight, and then took me to the bank. I was forced to fill a bag with money and hand it over to another one of the gang who arrived later.'

'That's awful,' I say, suddenly feeling as if I'm looking into this conversation from the outside. 'Did they get away with it?'

Mrs Collins again, 'One of them was killed, and they found some of the bank notes on his body. And two of the others were arrested. Ken had to ID them. Luckily, he has a very good memory for faces and voices, so they were convicted.'

'But they never got the one that I gave the money to,' continued Ken. 'That really bugs me sometimes.'

'But a lot of the money was found in France and returned, so the bank didn't lose much in the end,' says Mrs Collins.

'But we mustn't bore you with all of that,' says Ken, 'tell us about yourself.'

'Oh, my goodness, that must have been terrifying,' I mumble. 'I'm so sorry, but I must get back to work. Thanks for the drink.'

'Well, thanks for coming. We're off to lunch now, so probably see you later.'

'Yes, have a good lunch, and actually, you know, the Seaview Bar on the next deck is so much better than this one, but don't say I said so!'

'Oh, right ho, thanks.'

I'm drained. That poor old couple. And he retired early because of the robbery.

I'd like to go to lunch in a restaurant with Zak and tell him all about it, but he is classed as crew, while I'm staff, so he has to eat in the crew's mess, while I can go to the buffet.

So, I get enough for both of us, and we eat in our cabin. We feel like jumping ship. This is so risky. If Collins has such a good memory for faces and voices, Zak could come seriously unstuck. It may be a longshot, but it could happen.

It's uncanny. We go to Spain and the police turn up, we go to Antwerp and the cleaner from the adoption office appears, and then I bump into an ex-boyfriend on the Isle of Wight. And now this! I know it's a small world, but this is ridiculous. I'm half expecting Bunter and Cassie to appear at any moment! At least that would be a welcome sight. I wonder how they are.

Our next stop is the Canary Islands. If we seriously wanted to jump ship, it would be easy enough, but we haven't seen any more of the

Collinses, and we're both enjoying our jobs, so we decide to take the risk.

Zak says that they haven't been back to his bar, so he feels safer. I've seen them a couple of times from a distance but have managed to avoid them.

So, everything's okay.

Except it isn't.

At 2am, I'm practically thrown out of bed. The ship is rocking so much that it's hard to stand upright. My dressing gown is hanging on the cabin door at a 45-degree angle.

Even cool, calm Zak looks worried.

There's a lot of shouting going on, and I open the cabin door to investigate. A man wearing a life jacket rushes past and shouts to me to stay in the cabin and put on my life jacket. Now I'm scared. We both find life jackets under the bed and put them on after hastily getting dressed.

We sit and wait for a few minutes, and then Zak can't stand it. He has to find out what's going on. We both leave the cabin and stagger our way to the main central lounge.

A lot of passengers have gathered, some still in their night clothes. It's a dangerous place to be. A grand piano slides across the room and pins a woman to the wall. As the ship lurches again, a tea trolley loaded with crockery flies into a family group, smashing china and knocking a child to the floor.

Next, tables and chairs smash into the glass sides of the deck, and foul water starts to pour from a pipe in the ceiling.

There is no one from the crew to ask what's happening. We are in the middle of a storm and have no idea what to do.

Several people have been injured, and the smell of vomit is everywhere. People are shouting or crying or even praying.

Then the lights go out. We're in pitch blackness. The ship rears up again, and something hits me in the face. I have no idea what it is, but when I put my hand to my cheek, I can feel blood.

Suddenly, a man's voice shouts, 'Go to your cabins, and put your life belts on.'

Another, 'What's happening?'

'Just do it.'

'Listen to me, pal. I have a satnav with me, and we're miles off course. We should be docking in a few hours, and we're 24 hours from the Canaries!' shouts a voice from the darkness.

And another, 'Has the stabilising equipment failed?'

Then Zak, 'Great, we're lost in the middle of a storm with no stabilisers!'

With emergency lighting in the corridors, we manage to find our way back to our cabin.

I have a small cut just below my eye, but it's not much. It could have been much worse.

For the next couple of hours, the roar of the sea and the sound of people vomiting fills the air. Then, with a loud creak, a waste pipe above our beds starts leaking... how shall I put this… lavatory contents.

We're just about to head back to the main lounge when there's a knock on the door. A crew member with a clipboard asks for our names and writes them down. He tells us to stay put, and then he's gone before we can ask him anything.

'Bloody wonderful,' says Zak. 'Now what do we do?'

'Nothing we can do,' I say, trying to sound in control, but Zak knows me better than that.

He puts his arms around me. 'What a pair of losers we are,' he laughs. 'I reckon if we won the lottery, we'd lose the ticket!'

By the morning, the storm has passed, and the clean-up begins. We're moved to another cabin while pipes are repaired.

We decide that we've had enough, and that if and when we finally see land, we're off.

It's another twenty-seven hours before the ship limps into Las Palmas, Gran Canaria.

It seems a lot of others have the same idea as they struggle down the makeshift gangway with their luggage.

We watch as the gangway twists and turns and doesn't look safe at all. Far below it is the deep black harbour water.

Then there's a blood curdling scream. A woman walking down the rocky gangway has gone overboard.

One minute Zak's standing beside me, and the next, he's in the water. Huge crowds gather on the decks and on the harbour side. It was a long way to dive, but Zak soon has the woman with her head above water and is making for the dock. Crew members run to help him, and sirens start wailing as they get nearer.

As I try to run down the gangway, a crew member tells me not to risk it, but I don't care.

It sways under my feet, but I cling on, dragging our bags behind me.

Finally, the woman is dragged from the water, and Zac climbs from the sea up a metal ladder onto the harbourside.

There's pandemonium, and I rush to Zak. My totally deranged and dripping wet hero!

'That's one way to start the day,' he says.

'You are totally potty!' I say as I give him a hug.

We watch as the woman is loaded into an ambulance.

'Is she alright?' I ask.

'Yeah, just shocked, so was I when I saw who it was.'

Then we see Mr Collins rushing to the ambulance. He talks to someone who then points at Zak. Then he starts walking towards us.

'Oh no, he's coming over...disappear quick.'

Zak grabs a bag and rushes away in the opposite direction into the crowd. I casually pick up the other bag and start walking, but I'm too late.

Mr Collins rushes up to me.

'That man you were talking to, who is he?'

'Oh, I'm not sure, we just got chatting. He was fully clothed and dripping wet.'

'He saved my wife's life. It was amazing. She can't swim, you know, neither of us can. She would have drowned in seconds. He didn't hesitate; he was straight in!'

I shrug and smile. 'Is she ok?'

'Yes, they're checking her over now, but she's all in one piece.' He looks around for Zak. 'I must thank that man.'

'You go to your wife and send her my love. She needs you now, and I'm sure the man will show up again.'

Mr Collins smiles and rushes back to his wife.

Chapter Twenty-Three

I watch the ambulance take them both away and look around for Zak. I see him in a doorway at the far end of the harbour. I make my way over to him as the crowds disperse. He has changed into dry clothes but looks tired.

'That's another fine mess you got me into,' he says with a smile.

'Me!'

'What did Collins say?'

'He just wanted to thank that bloody man who just can't stop being a hero!'

'Did he ask who I was?'

'Of course. I said I didn't know, and that we'd only just got chatting.'

'Come on, we need to get out of here,' he sighs.

We grab our bags and trudge to the taxi rank. It's tempting just to get back on the ship and go to sleep in our cabin, but no doubt the Collinses will be back soon, and there'll be talk of the rescue, so we have to move on.

We get a taxi to the airport, which takes about half an hour in the traffic. Is it safe to use our passports again? We're too tired to care and don't know where we're going.

The first available flight is to Majorca. So, at least we get some food and a three-hour rest.

We have to take the only available seats, which puts me at the front and Zak at the back of the plane.

I have to sit sandwiched between a woman of about my age and a very old man.

He sleeps for the whole trip, and I'd like to, but the woman starts talking to me. She's Scottish but living in Majorca. I've never been, so I ask her about it. She loves it, she says. She moved out there when her husband died seven years ago, and as they had no children, she was free to take off. She makes her life sound idyllic.

Her name's Shona, and we chat happily for an hour or so before we both doze off.

I'm woken by Shona nudging me.

'We're about to land,' she says.

'Oh...ok, thanks.'

'I've been thinking,' she continues, 'As you've not planned where you're going to stay, why don't you come to my B&B? I have a room free for two weeks if that's any help. I charge about the same as everyone else, and as it's you, I'll throw in a cooked breakfast. Usually it's a Spanish style breakfast, bread, ham and cheese. What do you say?'

I'm trying to wake up. 'I'll have to ask my partner, but I'm sure that would be great. Thanks.'

The landing is uneventful, but I have white knuckles just the same, as I always do.

Once on the tarmac, I introduce Shona to Zak, and he's happy to go to her B&B. Even if we only stay for a night or two, it saves us having to find somewhere tonight. And she speaks English...well, sort of.

Majorca is achingly beautiful. I don't know why I haven't been here before. I think I've been put off by its Blackpool abroad image, you know, cheap packages for the hordes.

That's the snob in me. But I can now see why people come here.

Shona had left her car at the airport, so she confidently drives us through the back turnings until we come to her villa.

It's beautiful. White with arches and lemon trees in the garden.

Shona lives upstairs and lets out the self-contained flat on the ground floor.

It's better than the one room we'd expected. There's a room with a double bed, a room with two singles (great if we have a row, or Zak snores!), a kitchen, a bathroom and a sitting room. We pull back the curtains, and right in front of us is a private pool. It's surrounded by orange and pomegranate trees and to one side, a trellis with grape vines.

We can get a peek at the sea through the trees, but we can see why Shona lives upstairs. She must have a fantastic sea view.

We wander into the garden, and Shona calls from her balcony. 'Everything OK? Let me know if you need anything. What time would you like breakfast?'

'Everything's wonderful, thanks,' I call back. 'Breakfast at, say, nine?'

'Perfect,' says Shona. And with a smile goes back inside.

After a good night's sleep and a massive breakfast, we decide to go and explore the area.

Shona tells us there's a rastro today, a kind of boot sale/market near the beach.

Sounds great to me, but Zak says he'd rather go for a wander. We walk hand in hand to the rastro.

'I wonder who we'll bump into here!' says Zak.

'Shona's probably the chief constable of Cambridge!' I laugh.

He gives me a peck on the cheek and goes off for his walk. I'm more than happy to browse around the rastro.

The first thing I see is a cardboard box full of tiny puppies! An old man sits guarding them. On the side of the box is a handwritten sign saying E10. Ten euros.

I can't resist picking one up and giving it a cuddle. There are five of them, and they're all a creamy colour with a white blaze on their faces. The man speaks to me in Spanish, trying to sell me one, I suppose, but I just give him a smile and return the little furry bundle to the box of squeaking pups.

The rastro is fascinating. There are stalls selling secondhand stuff of every description and others with new clothes, especially pretty colourful dresses for little girls, and baby clothes.

I think of Gabriel. I wonder how he is and if he's being treated well. It's like a punch in the stomach every time I think of him.

The market seems to go on for miles. There are fruit and veg, some that I've never seen before; brightly coloured jumpers and T-shirts; white floaty dresses and sun hats.

I buy a wide-brimmed sun hat and get a coffee at one of the many coffee vans where seats are placed outside under the trees.

I love to watch the world go by. There are a lot of English voices and holiday makers of many nationalities. I feel at home here somehow.

I sit for an hour just taking in everything around me and then stroll back the way I came and eventually see the old man with the puppies. He's just holding one puppy up as if it were a potato and shouting something in Spanish. I look in the box. It's empty.

An English couple wander up beside me.

I look to them, 'Do you know what he's saying?' I ask.

'He's saying that this is the last one, and he will drown it today if no one wants it,' says the woman.

'He won't really, will he?' I'm shocked.

'Probably,' says her husband, 'they do that.'

The rastro is closing, and stall holders are packing up. The old man picks up the cardboard box and slings it into a nearby skip. For a moment, I think he's going to throw the pup in there with it.

'No!' I shout, 'I'll have him!'

I get ten euros from my purse and hand it to him. He thrusts the pup at me and walks away.

Well, what else could I do? I cuddle him to me and make my way back to Shona's place. Goodness knows what she's going to say.

On the way, I pass a pet shop and go inside.

The owner takes one look at the pup and says in very good English that he's too young to leave his mother. He's only about four weeks old.

I tell him what happened, and he said he wasn't surprised. He tells me to put the pup in a box in a cupboard so that he will feel secure… as if he were in a cave.

I find this strange but get some food for him and a collar and lead. He's mewling like a kitten. The man gives me a box, and I buy a dog blanket.

As I continue back 'home', I wonder what Zak will say. He'll think I'm mad, and of course, this is not the time to buy a dog, but I couldn't let him be drowned.

I decide to call him Chico.

When I get back, Shona is in the garden, trimming the glorious bougainvillea that climbs all over the white walls.

'Hi! I like the hat! What else have you bought?' she calls.

'Shona, I hope you won't be too cross, but I bought this little fella because they were going to drown him,' I hold Chico out to show her.

'Oh, the poor wee mite, just look at him! I've seen bigger hamsters! Good job you found him. I'll get you some newspapers for the floor...he'll be keeping you busy!'

'You don't mind?'

'Well, it won't be me cleaning up after him, so as long as everything's clean when you leave...and you take him with you, that's fine,' she grins.

'Thanks, Shona. Have you seen Zak?'

'Aye, he was here half an hour ago, but he went out again with two men.'

'Two men? He doesn't know anyone here.'

Chapter Twenty-Four

I go inside, put Chico into his box with a blanket, and phone Zak's burner. A man answers, but it's not Zak. I end the call in shock.

It rings. I gingerly answer it.

'Is that Verity Brown?'

'Who is this?'

'It's the police. Zak skipped bail and is wanted for questioning in the UK. We're taking him back.'

'Let me speak to Zak.'

'Ok but be quick.'

'Hi, sweetheart.' It's Zak.

'Zak, how did they find you?'

'Who knows. We've been using our passports, so I suppose it's not rocket science.'

'Are you okay?'

'I'm fine. What will you do? I think you should stay here and relax for a while.'

'No, I'll come back. I want to be with you.'

'You won't be able to be with me. I'll call you as soon as I get out. Keep that number.'

Then the voice of the policeman again, 'That's enough now. We may be wanting a word with you, Verity, so keep that phone with you. And don't disappear. These days it's impossible to go missing for long.'

With that, the phone goes dead.

I flop into the armchair. I suppose it was inevitable that this would happen, but I was feeling so safe.

They must have some evidence to arrest Zak and take him back. Surely, they wouldn't bother otherwise. My mind races through everything that's happened. What evidence could they have?

I feel so alone. I decide to ring Bunter. He knows the whole story, and he can support Zak until I get back.

'Verity, how the devil are you?'

'I'm fine, thanks, is everything ok there?'

'Great, thanks. I love your house, so you can't come back, ever, because I'm settled now.'

Typical Bunter. He always makes me smile.

'Bunter, Zak's been arrested. We only arrived in Majorca yesterday, and the police picked him up today. He's on his way back now.'

'Ah. That's not good. What have they got on him?'

'I've no idea, but I'm guessing they must have something.'

'Might just be a fishing trip. They have the excuse that he jumped bail.'

'Maybe. Is jumping bail a hanging offence?'

'Not sure, but they don't like you taking the pee.'

'Zak says he wants me to stay here because there won't be anything I can do and some sod's living in my house.'

'Probably best.'

'Can you keep in contact with the police and support him if possible?'

'Of course, if they'll let me.'

'You can get me on this number, and I'll get another burner so we can hopefully talk in private.'

'Ok, hun. I'll keep you posted if I hear anything. Try not to worry.'

'And, Bunter, could you please check on Cassie, Zak's sister? I'll text you her address. She only lives round the corner. And can you tell her about Zak?'

'Will do.'

The only good thing is that I know Zak can cope. Even if he gets sent to prison, it won't really faze him. His time in the army has prepared him for most things.

But if he goes away for a long time, it will kill me. Especially as it's all my fault. I got him into this whole thing with Chester, and that was the beginning of this madness.

But I mustn't think like that. He could be back here in a day or two. I must get a grip and get on with life.

Where's Chico? Little scamp is not in his box. I wander about looking for him, but there's no sign. I go outside just in time to see him toppling into the pool.

'No! Chico….'

I manage to grab him before he goes under.

I bought him to save him from drowning, and then almost drown him myself!

I sit at the edge of the pool cuddling him and crying. Shona appears on her balcony.

'Are you alright, hen?' I look up and give her a smile.

'Come up here and have a cup of tea with me. And bring the wee pup with you.'

I'm grateful for the company. Shona puts a pot of tea on the balcony table and brings out a coffee and walnut cake that's still warm. Chico scampers about in safety as the balcony wall is three feet high.

Her kindness and sympathy make me sob, and she is genuinely concerned.

'Come on, hen, nothing's that bad,' she says as she puts her arm around me.

Eventually, I tell her a version of events about Melody and Gabriel, and about Chester.

And that Zac has been arrested.

'Aye, I thought they were the poileas. You've had a bad time, lass.'

She cuts a large slice of cake and pours the tea.

'Nothing a bit of cake won't cure.'

As we sit in the sunshine eating cake and looking at the spectacular sea view, with a pup scampering about at our feet, it's hard to stay down for long.

Days pass with no news of Zak. I amuse myself by trying to train Chico, but he's too young. He just needs food, cuddles and sleep.

I'm aware that this place must be vacated in a few days as Shona has a booking. I don't know what to do. I doubt if many places will accept a puppy. And how would I get him home to England?

I cuddle him tight. I'm already in love with him.

My new burner rings. It's Bunter.

'They say no good deed goes unpunished,' he says.

'What?'

'Your heroic Zak has his picture all over the papers for saving that woman from drowning. The fact that he then disappeared has made it a good mystery story for the press. He was recognised by the ship's crew as a bartender, so his identity is no secret, but apparently, someone has picked him out for some skulduggery, and he's been remanded in custody.'

'What skulduggery? For how long?'

'That's all I know, pet. And I only know that thanks to my lawyer friend.'

'Oh, Bunter…'

'I know. Look, why don't you come home? At least you'll be able to visit him and get the full SP. I'll move out if you like. Or you could use my house in Cambridge.'

'I'll come back to my house if that's ok. You don't need to move out. I just want to be at home.'

'Of course.'

'Do you like dogs?' I ask.

'Love hot dogs.'

'Real dogs, you idiot!'

'Yes, I love dogs. Why?'

'I have the tiniest, sweetest puppy called Chico.'

'You're nuts. Can't wait to meet him. Let me know where and when you're arriving, and I'll pick you up.'

'Thanks, Bunter. Did you see Cassie?'

'I did. She's fine and sends her love.'

I discover that Chico needs a passport and rabies injection to travel, and that can take weeks or even months.

I invite Shona in for a cuppa and tell her all about it.

'No problem,' she says, bless her. 'You go on home and leave wee Chico with me. I'll get all his documents and jabs sorted and send him on to you.'

'Really? Would you do that? Can he travel alone?'

'Yes, yes and yes. No problem. My friend had to do the same thing with her cat.'

Chapter Twenty-Five

Bunter meets me at the airport with a big bunch of flowers, and a woman on his arm. It's Cassie!

We have a group hug, and I bite back the tears. I'd promised myself I wouldn't cry, but it's so good to be home. When did I become such a cry baby?

'What's all this, then?' I say as they hold hands.

Cassie grins all over her face and thrusts her ring finger at me. There sits a beautiful platinum and diamond ring.

'Flipping heck, you two. You work fast! Congratulations!'

'Not really, but thanks. We were keeping it a secret until you came home. We've been together for some time,' says Bunter, looking almost shy.

I'm delighted. They were both lonely, and they're two of my favourite people. Zak will be thrilled, his sister and his best friend...

Bunter decides to move in with Cassie. As he says, he spends most of his time there anyway when he's not working. So, I have my house back.

It feels as though I've come full circle. I'm back here on my own. Only I've lost my daughter, my grandson and my man, at least for now. I wander about feeling a bit lost. I make a cup of tea and sit down on the sofa.

The missing carpet is a reminder of that awful day with Chester. I have a flashback, and it all seems unreal.

All that money sitting in the bike shed. Chester's body under the tarpaulin. The pig farm, the woods. Blood on the carpet. Melody, the poor limp baby...

I can't stay here. I jump up, spilling my tea. I'm having a panic attack.

I run into the street, blinded by tears. I can't breathe. A car screeches to a halt, horn blaring.

I don't feel the impact.

Chapter Twenty-Six

When I wake, I'm in hospital with Cassie sitting beside me looking drawn.

'Verity, it's Cassie, can you hear me?'

I nod slightly. It hurts.

I start to panic again. Cassie calls the nurse, and then a doctor appears.

'Well, hello, sleeping beauty,' he says. 'You're okay. The nurse will give you something to calm you down. You've had a nasty bang on the head.'

I try to speak, but nothing comes out. Cassie wipes my lips with a damp cloth.

'You've been asleep for a long time. You're a hundred and five now! Just kidding.' I want to smile.

'Rest now, and we'll have a chat tomorrow.'

This morning, the nurse is helping me to sit up. Cassie has gone to get herself a sandwich.

It's painful to sit up, but I'm stuffed with pain killers, so it's bearable.

I notice someone sitting just outside the door. As I look, she glances at me and gets up. She comes into the room. It's a policewoman.

'Hello, Verity. Are you feeling better?'

I nod.

'Good. We were coming to your house to see you when you ran right out in front of our car.'

The police were coming to see me?

The doctor appears. 'Ah, sitting up, that's my girl. How are you feeling?'

I just nod. Somehow words won't come out.

'I think you have a special visitor,' he grins.

I look up and in walks Bunter carrying a dog the size of a spaniel.

'You have a dog?' I ask in a croaky voice.

'She speaks!' says the doctor. 'We'll come back after lunch,' he says as he guides the policewoman out.

Bunter smiles. 'He's your pup. Hasn't he grown?'

'No, I haven't got a dog.'

'Verity, you remember you bought a puppy in Majorca?'

'I've never been to Majorca.'

Bunter looks worried, and I feel panicked. What's he talking about?

My arm's in plaster, but I manage to stroke the dog's soft head. Then Bunter puts him on the floor, and the pup curls up and goes to sleep.

Bunter holds my hand. He looks at me with great affection in his eyes.

'You daft sod, trying to compete with a police car!'

I grin.

'I'm afraid they've thrown the book at Zak, sweetheart, but there are a lot of mitigating circumstances, so it might not be too bad.'

Thrown the book at Zak? Why?

I nod toward the policewoman sitting outside. 'Why is she here?'

'Not sure what the situation is there. Do you want me to bring her in to explain?' I nod.

He gets the woman, and she stands by the bed. Bunter offers her his seat, and she sits.

'I'm PC Morgan,' she says. 'If you're up to it, I'll explain the situation.'

'Yes, please.'

'Well, as you may know, Zak has been remanded in custody and is awaiting trial.

'Make no mistake, we have enough circumstantial evidence to charge you, too. But a view has been taken, bearing in mind what happened to your daughter and grandson, that you were also caught in the web of a violent man. And in view of your accident and subsequent injuries, the DPP has taken a lenient view. But we would like you to be a witness in the case against Zak.'

'Why, what's he done?'

'Ok, well we can talk about that later. The trial won't be for a few months yet. You just need to concentrate on getting better.' There is a pause, then she continues, 'Um, will you be making a complaint about the police car hitting you?'

I look at Bunter.

'I think Verity will need to discuss all this with her lawyer when she's up to it,' he says.

Good old Bunter.

Chapter Twenty-Seven

I'm finally at home and Bunter and Cassie are taking good care of me. The dog spends most of his time sitting beside me with his head on my lap. I think Bunter must have been teasing me about Majorca, but I like the dog he's given me. Bunter says he's called Chico.

You join me once again in the bath where I do my best thinking. In the tub.

Cassie is here to help me. And right now, I'm thinking, who knows, one day I might walk again.

They put Zak in prison, but I don't know why. He's such a nice lad. When they let him out, we'll have a fantastic party. My husband, James, likes Zac, so he'll be pleased to see him again. And Melody will be a teenager soon, so she'll enjoy a party.

It will be wonderful, won't it, Cassie?

About the Author

Suzanne Shearing is a retired journalist, stage school owner and film maker.

Starting on her local paper, the Welwyn Hatfield Times, as a cub reporter, she progressed to evening and national publications, writing news and features, as well as a local column.

In 1995 she had a change of career, due to her love of the theatre and film. After attending drama school, she opened a stage school, which soon became the most successful part time stage school in Hertfordshire, with 300 young students and fourteen teachers of drama, dance and singing.

When she retired, she started writing scripts, and made two feature films, 'No Smoke' and 'Archie', which have been distributed throughout the world, and a short, 'Nobody's Child.' 'No Smoke' was an official selection for the International Marbella Film Festival.

'That's a Shocking Idea… Let's Do It!' is Suzanne's second novel, her first being 'Two Old Ladies and a Secret Child', something she thought she would never achieve. Writing 80,000 words is not easy for a journalist who has been trained to keep everything short and sweet!

Suzanne lives in rural Hertfordshire with her pups Rusty and Rocky, and with her son and his family nearby.

She is working on her next novel with great enthusiasm, having discovered that fiction is so much more exciting than facts!

Suzanne would love to hear from her readers.

sueshearing@aol.com

www.suzanneshearing.com

Facebook - Two Old Ladies and a Secret Child

Printed in Great Britain
by Amazon